To Dad
Happy Birth

WINTER GEMS

Blasts of Bite Sized Fiction

WINTER GEMS

Published by WordPlay Publishing

www.wordplay-publishing.com

FOREWORD

In early 2010 a group of writers sat together for the first time to discuss the state of the publishing market, each other's hopes for their work and how their words, poems, and stories could get to market.

That group of writers has evolved during the intervening period, but the aim of the group has remained constant: to encourage writers to write, and then to get them read. And the encouragement that each member receives from their colleagues within the group has helped spur many to not only spread their wings in the genres in which they write, but to then go on and become published in their own right.

WordPlay's members have now published novels across several genres, as well as collections of poems, and anthologies of short fiction such as the one in your hands now.

We hope the reading of these stories gives you as much pleasure as the writing of them gave us.

iv

CONTENTS

BRIAN MIDWINTER'S JANUARY
Janette Davies

'Emergency. Which service?'

'Please. Please help me. I've killed somebody.'

'Putting you through to someone who will help you. Your name please.'

'It's January, January...er...January.'

'Hello January, my name is Anne, I'm here to help you.'

'Please. Please. I am so sorry. I didn't mean to kill him but he wouldn't let me go. He kept pulling at me and he hurt my knee. He pushed me and I fell on the bed. I just grabbed something and I hit him with it I didn't mean to kill him, I just wanted him to stop it.'

'Okay January, what is this person's name?'

'Dom, Dominic. He's a footballer.'

'Is Dominic your boyfriend?'

'No, I only met him tonight at the club.'

'Which club?'

'Foxy Lady in Braxton.'

'Where exactly are you now January?'

'In the sitting room.'

'Where is Dominic now?'

'In the bedroom.'

'What is Dominic's surname?'

'I don't know.'

'Do you know the address where you are?'

'No. It's a flat but I don't know whereabouts it is.'

'Right, when you went into the flat was Dominic wearing a coat or jacket?'

'A leather jacket, it's there on the back of a chair.'

'Look in his pockets and see if you can find a wallet

or something with his name and address on - his driving licence or bank cards.'

'There's nothing in his pockets. Hang on, yes there's a credit card.'

'What's the name on it?'

'Dominic H. de Lane There's nothing else No driving licence or anything. When we came out of the club, Lex'an said that we would stay together but his friend wouldn't get in Dominic's car. She pushed me in the car and then walked off and started kissing his friend. I could see them laughing; laughing and waving at me. She went - went off with him and left me. I tried to get out of the car but Dominic'd locked the doors. I couldn't get out and now I don't know where I am. She promised me we would stay together and I am really scared. I'm sorry if I'm not making sense but she promised if I went with her we would stay together.'

'January, try not to get upset. I really need you to stay strong and focused so we can find you and get you out of there. What is your full name and address?'

'It's January, J-A-N-U-A-R-Y, er, er, I can't, can't, I can't remember the rest of my name Anne, I CAN'T REMEMBER MY NAME.'

'Keep calm January. Is January your real name or did you make it up?'

'No, it really is my name. Lex'an said that nobody at the club would believe that it was really my name but it is. My dad said that when I was born I had lots of pure white hair that looked like snow on a hillside. Because I was born in the January, he really wanted to call me 'Snowdrop' but my Mum wouldn't let him Obviously, I'm really glad about that. Fancy being called Snowdrop. Sorry. I'm, er, rambling on.'

'Don't worry, your dad sounds nice, what's his name?'

'Brian, Brian Midwinter. He died last year and my Mum's finding it really hard on her own, that's why we moved here to be nearer my Nan. Oh God! My name's Midwinter, January Midwinter and I live at 12 Oaks Drive, Braxton. How could I forget my own name?'

'It's because you've had a shock, its quite a com...'

'Anne, ANNE, it's BELVEDERE COURT that's where I am. It had Belvedere Court in big silver letters on the wall by the lift. That horrible man was standing in front of the sign when he pressed the button. He kept sniggering and he said 'Nice one Dom, scored again I see.' Dominic threw his car keys to him and he said 'Park it for me Rich,' and he smirked and said 'Yes sirree, Romeo's Romeo - CONSIDER IT PARKED,' winked and did a stupid little salute. The car, yes, the car I know it's an Alfa Romeo, it's black and the inside's red and smells like new leather.'

'Well done. Who is this man, Rich?'

'A sort of doorman - he was wearing a brown uniform with a hat and he had a beautiful black dog with a big collar: it had 'Inky' on it.'

'That's excellent January, well done. Do you remember if there was a number on the door to Dominic's flat?'

'No, 'cos Dominic kept trying to kiss me in the lift. He had his arm round my waist, it was so tight I could hardly breathe and he kept pulling at the straps on my dress. After he'd opened the front door, he virtually threw me in the room and he ripped my dress. My heel caught in the rug and I tripped and fell on the coffee table. I've cut my knee. It's not even my dress, it's

Lex'an's - she'll be furious.'

'January, what school do you go to?'

'Braxton High. Why?'

'How old are you?'

'Er… 17 next year.'

'So, when are you 16?'

'Two weeks' time, on the 19th'

'So, at the moment you are 15, correct?'

'Yes.'

'Did you give false ID to get in the Foxy Lady?'

'Oh, no Lex'an goes there every week and she says that if you wear a very short dress the bouncers are too busy looking at your legs to bother with ID.'

'So this was your first visit and presumably your friend's dress was short enough to allow you to get in. Does your mom think you are staying at Lex'an's house tonight?'

'Yes, I thought I was I thought we would go home together I've never been to a Night Club before, but Alexandra said that..'

'Who's Alexandra?'

'Oh, that's Lex'an's proper name, she's Alexandra O'Neal, but she likes to be called Lex'an with an 'apostrophe'. Anyway, she goes every week and gets drinks from footballers, 'cos that's where they go after they've played on Saturdays. She says that she's, er, gone with lots of them because they always buy champagne, She thinks I've, er, done it as well, but I haven't; honestly I haven't. I let her think I had 'cos I didn't want to appear stupid but I haven't. I know you are going to tell my Mum but it's not her fault. It's the first time I've ever told her a lie and I only did it because Lex.., I mean Alexandra, kept on telling me to get a life.'

'Everything is going to be alright, January. We know where you are and we are on our way now. We'll be there in about three or four minutes. Your Mom and your Gran know where you are and they will be waiting for you when we get you safe. Go to the front door now and wait there. When we come in, go straight to the Policewoman and give your phone to the Sergeant. Is that clear? Not long now, we are nearly there.'

'Yes I'm ever so sorry but I told him I wasn't doing it with him. I kept telling him to stop but he didn't. If he'd stopped, I wouldn't have hit him I didn't mean to ki…….NO!! YOU CAN'T BE ALIVE. NO!! GET AWAY FROM ME GET AWAY FROM ME ANNE, ANNE. PLEASE HELP ME!! HE'S ALIVE. HE'S COMING TO GET ME. THIS CAN'T BE REAL.'

'January, January, can you hear me? Go to the door now. We are outside the door. Go to the door now. Go to the Policewoman.'

'I've pushed him. I've pushed him. He's on the floor. There's blood everywhere.'

'WILLIAMS HERE!!'

'Anne Baxter ACC. What's the situation Sergeant?'

'Ma'am? Er, good evening Ma'am. Er, well, he's not dead. He's copped a wallop with the proverbial blunt instrument but he'll live. Paramedics are looking at him now.'

'Good. I think she hit him with a bedside lamp. What does the girl look like?'

'Stunning bird, begging your pardon Ma'am. 'Bout six foot tall, usual bottle blonde. Dress, what there is of it, virtually ripped to shreds. My Betty's got vests longer than that dress No wonder these girls get themselves into trouble.'

'I meant injuries, Sergeant.'

'Sorry Ma'am. Bad cut on her leg - paramedics are dealing with it now, think it'll need a stitch or two. Bad scratches on her shoulder, it looks like bruises round her neck, and I reckon she'll have a right shiner tomorrow.'

'Right, get everyone down the Station Go easy on the mother and grandmother, they've had a tough 12 months already, without all this. Let the girl see them - I'll take personal responsibility for that. Tell our Sporting Hero to get his Solicitor down the Nick because he's going to need him.'

'What are we charging him with?'

'Kidnap, assault, attempted rape, driving whilst disqualified. That'll do for starters. Another thing, Sergeant, get Miss Stephanie 'Foxy Lady' Laurenston down to the Station pronto; I'd like a quiet word with her about the age of a certain Miss O'Neal and her classmates.'

'Yes, Ma'am. Ma'am, d'you think we'll make it stick this time? I mean, we've pulled him in before but the girls always back down and won't press charges.'

'Oh yes, Sergeant, I reckon we've got him this time. He picked on the wrong one with Brian Midwinter's January.'

SHATTERED
Nikki Dee

Pete Mooney closed his lap top and prepared to leave the office, calling out to his boss as he went. 'Just off now Alan, see you tomorrow.'

'Make sure you tie this lead down,' Alan shouted back. 'You need a few decent sales this week Pete. I'm doing my best to help you out mate, but I can't keep you on if you don't bring something decent to the table pretty soon.'

'No worries, I'll pull this one off.' Pete said, as he made a dash for the lift before Alan could see the sweat he was certain was beading on his brow. He hated having to lie about leads to Alan but what the hell else could he do. He groaned and slumped once he reached his car, he couldn't see any way forward at the moment. He was being pushed from pillar to post at the moment, patching up here, bluffing there and all the time trying to be good old Pete. Smiling and coping. Truth was he didn't think he even remembered good old Pete. It had been such a long time since he'd done anything except struggle to keep going one day at a time.

He drove to the school and parked with minutes to spare and, by the time Nell came out with half a dozen other little girls all giggling and skipping, he'd calmed himself down. This is the important thing he reminded himself. This matters, nothing else comes close.

His daughter saw him and squealed as her eyes lit up. 'Daddy, daddy, guess what we did today.' She raced towards him and launched herself into his arms, trusting that he'd catch her, as he always had. He swallowed a lump in his throat. He would catch her, always.

'Tell me in the car princess. We're in a hurry because someone has a birthday party to go to I seem to remember.' They chattered and teased each other all the way home and Pete felt himself remembering what happiness was all over again. Once home they began the all important process of deciding what Nell would wear to the party.

'Daddy, I want to wear my pink dress and the trainers with butterflies on, I think.'

Pete only gave one suggestion and was told, in a quite stunningly patronising tone, that at his age, and being only a man, he really didn't know what he was talking about. He bowed to her superior knowledge and, in due course, drove her to the nearby burger bar. Evidently no self-respecting seven year old could or would even consider holding a party anywhere else.

Nell ran straight in and vanished into a huddle of squeals and screams. He turned away realising he'd been dismissed and smiled as Susan the organising mother moved toward him.

'Hi Pete, long time, no see. How are you?'

'Getting better every day, thanks Suze. Look, sorry but I have to dash off, a lot to get done in my hours of freedom, you know?'

'I know, I know. You go on, I'll hang on to her until you get back.' Susan smiled sadly at his almost indecent haste to get away. It was her own fault, she'd tried once, clumsily, to let him know if ever he needed a shoulder to cry on he only had to call. The poor guy went white and has never stood still in her company since. They used to be such good friends, before he got mixed up with that vile woman. He seemed to change, became almost a shadow of the man that he'd been. Susan had always had a major crush on him but he never noticed. Then when he had found out, he was obviously horrified.

Pete was already drawing away as he thanked her, reviewing all he had to accomplish in the next three hours: Pick up a pre ordered piece of glass and fix bathroom window. One load of laundry on the line and another in. Run around with the hoover. He thanked the gods of commerce for all night supermarkets. He could shop on the way home with Nell. Shopping bills were much higher when she came with him but somehow even Tesco's in December became almost magical when shared with Nell.

He reached home at last and switched on the kettle and the answer machine at the same time. There was a hesitant message from Mum confirming they would be home tomorrow, she also said she'd ring again later as she didn't trust the machine.

He'd be sorry in a way to see the end of this week alone with Nell, but this was his parents' home after all. He was so grateful that they'd made room for him and Nell, just at a time when they were quite rightly relishing their retirement and freedom. To be fair his parents made them both so welcome he truly thought they were enjoying the cramped conditions and the profusion of pink plastic that now dominated their previously beige house.

The phone rang as he was upstairs getting ready to replace the pane of glass and he only just got to it just before the machine kicked in. He heard a strangers voice, not his Mother's as he'd expected.

'Hello Mr Mooney, my name is Gibson, Dr Gibson.

I've been working with your wife, she may have mentioned me?'

'I have no contact with my wife. At all. Why are you calling me?'

'Ah well, it's a bit sensitive.'

'Dr Gibson, I have no interest in, or contact with, my wife. Tell me what you want, or go away. I don't really care. Just do it quickly.'

'Oh sorry. Yes. Well, um, your wife seems to have, um, gone missing in fact.'

Pete sank to the floor, as that familiar sick feeling washed over him. He felt the hot shame of powerless fear again.

'What the hell do you mean missing, how, when?'

'She went shopping this morning, all perfectly normal. She hasn't returned yet, I'm certain there's no problem but protocol demands that I notify you...

'Protocol demands that you should be keeping raving bloody lunatics locked up. What the hell do you mean, she went shopping. Are you aware that she almost killed me and our daughter. Deliberately. And you let her go shopping alone.'

'Mr Mooney, I'm calling you because I'm required to do so. The police have been informed and we are confident that your wife will be safely returned to us in no time.'

'I admire your confidence. Have you even read her file, I mean are you actually aware of what she's done?'

'She's been having treatment now for three years. She's calmer and more positive than I've ever known. She'll be quite safe I'm sure.'

'You absolute bloody cretin, It's not her safety that's the issue.' Pete forced himself to stop shouting, and then continued to explain to this incredible moron just what he meant. 'When my daughter was three years old that woman beat her to within an inch of her life. She'd been abusing her for three years and I didn't know. She then gave a false statement to the police, and stood by as I was arrested for child abuse. My career was gone, most of my friends were gone and my daughter almost died. It was only my daughters evidence that eventually cleared me. When the truth came out she stood in court and vowed to kill me and my child, she swore she wouldn't rest until we were both dead.

This is the woman you let go shopping. Christ man you should be under lock and key yourself.'

As he slammed down the phone in frustration the doorbell rang. The police had received the report and were following up. 'Is your daughter here with you Sir.'

'Oh Christ no. She's at a birthday party. I must go.' He jumped up and reached for his car keys.

'Tell us where she is Sir, we can radio out quicker than you'll get there.'

He gave them the address and Susan's phone number and then sat and made deals with God until word came through that Nell was safe and well. She was being escorted to a police car and would be safely delivered home. She was now the envy of all the other little girls.

'We'll leave a car outside for the rest of the day Sir, but I don't think there's any real cause for concern. It appears that your wife has been having a day out a week for six months and has given no sign of trying to get away. Get in touch if you're worried though. At any time.'

Pete made his way upstairs to the bathroom trying

to pull himself together. Nell thought he was superman and he couldn't let her see him as he was right now. A tearful weak failure. A salesman who struggled every week just to keep on basic wage, the world of high bonus or commissions was not his world. A man who had disappointed his wife.

He was the man whose unhappy wife became so bitter at an unwanted pregnancy she took her bile out on him. The screaming and the spite were shocking to him but the violence, when it started, was absolutely devastating. How could he defend himself against her, he'd never hit a woman, pregnant or otherwise. And she was terrifying when she became angry. But he couldn't leave her, she was carrying his child.

He remembered telling himself that when the baby was born things would improve. Meanwhile he kept quiet, tried to do his job and to keep her happy and whilst moving heaven and earth to prevent his parents from finding out the truth about his toxic marriage. She never stopped abusing him but did seem to dote on Nell. Nell, who had instantly lit up his world.

As he leaned over the sink to splash cold water on his face he saw in the mirror the door behind him open and suddenly he sensed her presence.

She came in screaming. 'You ruined my life you pathetic bastard, I'll kill you.' A knife was in her raised hand and was coming down fast.

No time to think. He grabbed the pane of glass that was waiting to be fitted and let her hand, holding the knife hit it. The knife bounced as the glass cracked. He took a breath and swung blindly with the remaining half pane. He felt it hit home and heard her sigh as she slipped to the floor.

He wiped her blood and his tears from his face and called the police. At last the fear had left him.

THOSE SIMPLE WORDS
Peter Hayward

Tom was shivering. Not because of the snow-filled, freezing weather of the dark, moonless night at minus nine degrees for he was acclimatised to it now, but shivering from the fear racing through his mind – the fear of loss. It was his bottle of cider, not theirs.

His bottle meant the world to him. Without it he would be helpless. Without it he would panic. Without it he wouldn't survive. That bottle, at this time in his life, was his lifesaver.

'Don't,' he shouted in a slurred, indecipherable voice.

But no one listened. No one heard.

He tried to hug his bottle, but a brown high-laced booted foot swung and kicked it away. He stretched to grab it but it had rolled out of his reach. A kid from a passing group of teenagers sniggered as the bottle repeatedly rotated along the footpath. From his prone position in the shop doorway, Tom stretched towards his bottle, but, yet again, the bottle was booted out of his range.

The shop had always offered Tom sanctuary, but now it was gone. It was yet another victim of this cruel, crazy world. It used to be his shop. Not his from being an owner or an employee, but his because it was the only place where he felt safe enough to seek out the now guiding force of his life – alcohol. It had been a place where he could get his fix, a place where he could get some comfort from people who had some understanding and pity for him. A place where he was accepted for what he was. But now the shop was closed. It was no more. Everything had disappeared, just like his past life: all gone!

Gone was the man who had shared a wonderful but brief time with his amazing, caring wife. Gone, the fit and able, hard-working individual, the seasoned golfer and amateur footballer he once was. Gone, the dependable man who was always prepared to help, offer advice and give guidance to anyone who sought his counsel. Gone was the man who would have given a vagrant lying in a doorway, just like he was now, a little money to help him.

If anyone had brought their issues to him, he had been a person who felt that he should make them feel valued, and not worthless. Their issues were important to them. He knew that were he to judge that person, deny their issues were important, or regard them lightly, they might not seek his counsel again. They had had the courage to approach him and he had the responsibility to hear them.

Tom looked down at his calloused and dirty, wrinkled cold hands, ragged and blackened by months of not washing. His clothes, once new and freshly laundered, were now worn and torn by the roughness of their use. His overcoat, recently taken from a rubbish bin, was too big for him, but with sleeves rolled up, it offered some protection from the kid with the brown high-laced boot that kicked him again. The cardboard he lay on was cold and damp from the frozen ground. An infested and rotten blanket covered his legs. A plastic bag, containing only a photograph, fluttered in the slight breeze.

The hands of the church clock silently moved towards five-thirty in the morning, and Tom shivered again.

'What am I doing?' Tom mumbled to himself.

'He's shivering,' shouted one of the kids. 'Let's set fire to his bed. That'll warm him up.'

'Nah,' said another. 'That's a waste of a match.'

The group of kids were bunking off from the local authority home for the umpteenth time. They made their fun that night by taunting him. Kids who had no parents. or who had been kicked out of their homes because of their selfish, intolerant or belligerent behaviour. Kids who thought they knew it all. No one could tell them anything. No one could tell them what to do. They knew their rights and they knew they couldn't be corrected or chastised. Kids who were now acting like pack animals.

But, like Tom, they were also victims. Victims of themselves. Victims of poor or no parenting. And victims of the system. The system that stated it would do lots, but, in effect, did very little.

Why were these kids angry? Were they, like Tom, in denial? Were their feelings, their hurt, their anger from their respective previous lives subconsciously hidden? Who could tell? They couldn't, unlike Tom, who'd had some experience and knowledge of the pain of life. Perhaps one day those kids might recognise and understand their own inner pain, their inner scars that were in need of healing.

But, not even Tom was ready to understand that unexpressed feelings of anger and hurt were perhaps the most difficult feelings to face. The kids possibly

16

had similar early lives of being unable or not allowed to express their emotions, so, to gain a sense of control, they engaged in punishing those around them, unknowingly blaming others for their issues, trying to gain a sense of power over others, just as they were now over Tom. Little did they know that this power only gave them a temporary reprieve from their pain and suffering and only a momentary feeling of satisfaction. Little did they, or Tom, know that what they were all actually doing was delaying facing their pain. They were in denial. But something was happening to Tom; something was stirring inside of him.

'I am someone,' he mumbled, before those voices inside his head returned. Voices that triggered fear mixed with those feelings of repressed anger, which left him so powerless to stick up for himself. His mind ruthlessly chuntered away. It was his cider bottle, not theirs. HIS.

Tom's mind came back into focus.

'Parents,' Tom mumbled.

'What,' snarled one of the kids.

A female voice!

'A girl,' Tom muttered, and a painful thought crossed his mind.

He stifled the voices and memories came back.

'She died before we had a little girl. She always wanted a baby girl,' Tom garbled, but his mind raced away again as he tried to reach for his bottle, his comforter, his pacifier.

The brown high-laced boot lashed out at him, provoking a terrifying pain. Tears filled his eyes. He tried to focus. He could see a woman with a baby and he reached out, but he couldn't touch them. Suddenly he saw his bottle again and he lunged towards it, but he couldn't touch it either. He couldn't hold it; he couldn't hug it. He cried out.

The kids just laughed and mocked him even more.

Tears and searing pain welled up inside Tom's body.

'Where are your parents?' he bawled.

'Nothing to do with you, you scabby tramp,' the boy with the brown high-laced boots shouted with sheer hatred that dripped from every word like venom from a snake.

'Why? Why me?' Tom questioned, before racing, panicking thoughts of fear - so much fear - returned again as he caught sight of his bottle just out of his reach.

Tom had dropped out of life some years ago. It had something to do with the wiring of his brain. Something took him and he didn't know what. Although on the outside, Tom had been a good man, inside he was lonely, depressed and sullen, with a deep-seated anger in his subconscious. An anger that he had unconsciously developed and unknowingly allowed to fester away inside his mind, driving his every depressing and negative thought. Anger he couldn't see. Anger he didn't want to see. An anger which now controlled him.

During his early childhood years, voices, planted and continually reinforced by his father, and never contradicted by his mother, told him he was a failure; told him he was no good; told him he was useless. No matter how hard he tried. And he had tried.

These harmful thoughts had affected the wiring of his brain. They had left him with low self-esteem and an eternal search for something. Someone to love him. He didn't know how to love himself and so sought someone to love him unconditionally. Seeking that unconditional love became his addiction

Eventually, Tom met, as he thought, the one and only person capable of loving him. A wonderful person, who was willing to listen to him, a person who wanted to be with him, a person who cared for him, a person who gave him affection and who gave him attention. Jacquie.

Jacquie became his addiction. She gave him the love and pleasure he sought and soon she became his wife. After a few years they had a child, a boy. But Jacquie had always wanted a baby girl. She quickly became pregnant again, but during the birth, Jacquie was tragically taken from this world together with their stillborn daughter.

Tom tried to raise his son, Jack. But Tom couldn't cope. He had never been given any instructions on how to cope. He had never been taught the necessary skills to bring up a child on his own. He just didn't know what to do. He struggled for years until Jack was eventually taken away. Tom then left his world for another world. Alcohol!

Alcohol had always been part of his life – the odd drink with his mates or the glass of wine with his wife. Alcohol made him feel good. But the wiring of his brain that forced his search for 'that special love' to give him pleasure had forced him to search for that pleasure through alcohol. And he drank. Alcohol became his addiction.

19

The longer he drank, the more he felt its pleasure. And the more he drank, the more the alcohol forced its poison into his brain. Alcohol forced its own thoughts and its own justification. The primitive human instinct of hunter-gatherer gave in to the search for alcohol for his most basic needs. Alcohol provided all that he required. Alcohol created a new vision for him. Now he saw his world through his bottle.

Tom's mind came back into focus for the search of his bottle. He groaned in self-pity and pain, and a rising anger. The sound of the girl had stirred something in the deep recesses of his mind. Something someone from Social Services had once said to him, which he had ignored at the time, came to the forefront of his mind. 'When you are ready, you will understand.'

His mind had dismissed this statement because he wasn't ready but now something inside of him was igniting. Little sparks of information were slowly coming back. He started to remember things. Jacquie, a baby girl – they had both died. But where was the boy? What happened to the boy?

Tom was realising only he had the answers to his pain. Only he could ease his suffering. Only he could help himself. He was getting ready.

'What have I denied?'

Denial had protected Tom from his pain and it had also rendered him blind to his feelings, his needs and his wants. It was like a thick blanket that smothered him. It hid the reality of the pain of his early childhood that continued through his whole adolescent life and well into adulthood. It hid the reality of his addictions; the need to seek someone to love him because he didn't know that he could love himself. Loving himself was important. Tom didn't know that with self-love came self-worth, inner confidence and inner belief.

His life had always been full of blinkered approaches to everything. He just thought 'This is how my life is and will always be.' And, in part, life had participated in these processes. Using denial, he lost touch with reality, his feelings, and himself. He joined in with those harmful experiences without even knowing it. There was so much denial that had his blanket had been ripped from him, he knew he would die from the shock of the exposure. But now he was catching a glimpse of the awareness of his pain, of his feelings, of his behaviour. He was beginning to understand, beginning to recognise. He was beginning to own his own power. He was on the path to recovery.

Tom's eyes were starting to open to the world.

'Where's my boy?' Tom pleaded out loud, but no one answered because, again, no one was listening to him

He reached for his bottle but brown high-laced boot brutally kicked, and Tom slumped to the ground in agony. Something sparked in his brain; he could take no more. His frail body, so brittle after years of under-nourishment yet fed regularly with alcohol, was now easily damaged. Years of negative thoughts, self-pity, running away instead of facing his truth, now festered away inside of him like a pressure cooker with the valve jammed shut. He needed to release that valve; he needed to confront his life. He began to realise that only he could do it, no one else could. His brain needed rewiring. Tom didn't know but he was getting ready to take that blanket off himself. For the first time in his life he was ready to fight. Fight the pain that he had allowed to be inflicted on him. The pain he had stifled to appease others. He was ready to stand up for his own values, his own wants and his own needs. He was ready to confront the pain he had denied for so long.

Tom slowly moved.

'I am me,' he shouted, with an almost wolf-like howl.

The drive for freedom, from the torture of these thugs and the torture of his life, momentarily hid his pain. He rolled over and lay on his back staring up at the dark, cloudless sky.

Stars! He could see so many stars shining brightly down on him.

'Is this heaven?' he wondered.

But the stars were slowly fading as the early morning sun was trying to peek over the distant horizon.

Suddenly, his upper body was lifted up by the collar of his coat. He stared into the eyes of the boy. It was the boy with the high-laced brown boots that had been inflicting the pain. The boy, who, at that moment, had a fist clenched ready to punch him.

Like a switch turning on a light, something clicked in Tom's head. A glimmer of brightness partially cleared the smog in his thoughts as a shivering, tingling sensation travelled up his spine. A strange feeling entered his mind, a feeling he'd only experienced when he was with Jacquie. A slight buzz made him smile. A clearing of his thoughts silenced the internal voices in his head. A sliver of confidence returned and Tom's self-worth grew. The dawn of the new day heralded the dawn of a new Tom. Tom was realising that he had accepted the misery in his life, and, furthermore, he had clung to it because it was something he knew so well and felt comfortable with. But, he was recognising he needed to change. Change meant changing his whole thought process and what he believed about his life. That would be hard, but he remembered he had a son, Jack. What had happened to Jack? Why had he deserted Jack? Why had his parents not given him the necessary life skills? Tom's mind started racing away again. This time, though, the negative voices were replaced with questions. Questions he'd left unanswered, questions that now needed resolving. Only he could answer them. Tom was now ready.

Tom stared straight into the boy's angry, contorted face.

There was a moment of silence as puzzled expressions hit both of them. A few seconds passed. Then recognition in both of their eyes!

'Jack? Jack!'

'Dad? Dad! It can't be?' Why dad? Why?'

Tom opened his arms and hugged the boy mumbling, 'I'm sorry son, I'm so, so sorry.'

Those simple words, and actions, were what Tom had dreamt of receiving from his father but never had.

In each other's arms they both cried.

THE CHEST
Joy Lennick

'Goodnight then, Tanya. Sleep tight!' Tanya felt a frisson of ill ease –not exactly fear – she had battled that emotion. Or had she? As editor of the very popular 'The Gentle Sex?' magazine, and used to being in charge, she wanted to scream from frustration. Fate, bad luck, whatever…had stepped in and she couldn't do a bloody thing about her situation. Though hardly comparable to her present predicament, she had edited enough crime stories about imprisoned women somehow escaping, so what was stopping her from waiting until he was asleep and leaving? A bloody dodgy ankle, that's what!! She let out a breath of angry air.

'Tom' had given Tanya a few of his absent sister's magazines to read before sleeping – where was she, she wondered? Normally a fairly sensible woman, why was she jumping to so many ridiculous conclusions; asking internal, unanswerable questions? 'Pull yourself together, Tanya – you're thirty, not thirteen!' her inner voice chided. She thought back to earlier in the day…

The words 'We all live in a yellow submarine, a yellow submarine, a yellow submarine,' were, fortunately for any canine creature around, trapped in the fiery red Lotus Tanya was driving towards Hay-on-Wye. Happiness suffused her being She thought that she would burst she was so happy…She couldn't have answered why she chose the Beatles song. Maybe because it had such a jaunty lilt which suited her carefree mood. Tanya – elfin-faced and bodied – her green eyes sparkling, glanced at the glittering diamond solitaire ring adorning her left hand ring finger, and lifted her shoulders briefly, like a little girl given her first red balloon. To think that darling, while slightly conservative, Justin could be so impetuous…

They had been out shopping for groceries when the rain started.

'Let's shelter in this doorway,' he had said. And before she knew what time of the day it was, she found herself faced with a dazzling array of rings under a pristine glass case. No preamble, no clues…no proposal – just 'Pick one, Tan…' She heard herself repeating 'Pick one?'' incredulous at such a suggestion. Justin didn't, after all, believe in commitment, well not of the marriage variety. He had said so, several times. Her head had felt that it was under water; she had to hold on to a counter to steady herself. Was that really only two days ago?!

Tanya and Justin had been 'an item' for over three years. Everyone said they were 'So suited!' But, being a cautious, ponderous sort of guy, it had taken him over a year to broach the subject of moving in together. And now – out of the blue, and completely out of character - he had bought the ring and suggested 'Let's not wait any longer, Tan – fancy shacking up for, say, fifty years?' Over the moon, she had replied: 'Don't know about fifty…will forty-nine do?' Ever since, there had been a whirlwind of plans, dates and arrangements, the first being a visit to Tanya's parents in Hay-on-Wye to spring the surprise news. She was on her way there now; Justin planning to arrive a day later due to a 'Sheik rattle and roll, ha ha, arriving to buy that five mil. property in Weighbridge, Surrey tomorrow, wouldn't you know! Sod's law.' Knowing that if he clinched the sale, the bonus would be a generous one, Tanya said:

'Hail Sod!'

Tanya's mood sobered a little as she glanced at the sky: ominous, metallic grey storm clouds were gathering. Umm. Fifty miles to go! Rain spattered against the windscreen: light at first, then gathering in intensity – a sudden gusty wind whipping it to battle with the wipers. Damn having to work this morning, she thought, mindful of the failing light. Still, she had faith in her red jalopy to get her to her old home safely. Wedding plans started filling her head, taking her mind off the increasing obstinacy of the storm. Strains of the bridal march, followed by the heart-squeezing Ave Maria, filtered in, until an almighty crash brought her rudely to the present and her brain properly into gear. Within a split second, her car had literally crunched into an immoveable mass, which proved to be a large fallen tree.

'Oh God!' she yelled instinctively; her body and head jolting forward; her seat belt saving her from serious injury. Nevertheless, her neck hurt and the steering wheel had bruised her chest. Gathering her senses, she told herself not to panic, that these thing happened, and that at least she was in one piece, with not a drop of blood in sight. What to do first: ring the AA, the police, or her parents? She dismissed the last course of action, while rummaging in her bag for her mobile. Once found…Nothing. Silence. 'Damn, oh damn…I didn't charge it up! You silly, silly cow!' she chided herself, pummelling a fist on the steering wheel. Peering into the semi darkness – there was a full moon

– she gave a grateful sigh, hating the denseness of a stark winter's night. The rain had abated a little, even though the fierce wind was still tossing torn branches about as if matchsticks. With no useful phone, and stuck in an area naked of houses, but boasting myriad trees and bushes, she appealed to a higher hand to help her. None came. Since her car was uselessly wedged in timber, even though the immediate area was deplete of evident life, she made a decision to leave the car and seek help. There, surely, would be a car or vehicle of some kind along shortly? And, around the next corner, a cottage? Perspiration marked her palms.

As she left the car, grabbing an anorak with a hood from the back seat, plus a pair of gloves, her bag and a torch – she appealed to her inner voice for courage.

'You're going to be all right, Tanya. Believe it!' it said, while she shivered in the biting cold. The moon cast eerie, intermittent shadows through the trees, making her shrink further into her clothes.

'Best foot forward now…watch your step…!' With the words hardly out of her mouth, Tanya tripped over a hidden log and fell headlong in the mud muttering 'Shit, shit, shit…' pulling herself up by holding onto a stronger, more protected sapling in the roadside wood. With her casual shoes and ankles covered in mud, she winced as she tried moving forward; one ankle having twisted in the fall. Adding a few more expletives, she hobbled on, while pathetically attempting to wipe the mud off her gloves, anorak and chin with a tissue from her pocket.

'Calm down. Someone's bound to come along soon,' her inner voice assured. No-one did. She was finding the pain hard to bear but couldn't give up. She hobbled on. Surely there would be a light in a window around the next bend, she thought. There wasn't. Tears were near but she told them to sod off.

'You're made of stern stuff, Tanya, remember that!' Her ex-Army father's words came to her, declared after her pet cat, Fluffy, had died. They were all very well, at the time, as she had someone to comfort her then! Minutes ticked by, and then – when, despite all, tears threatened to fall - she heard a car in the distance. She shone her torch on the road, and a silver Peugeot 307 slowed down and stopped. Tanya gave a heartfelt sigh of relief. A tall, thin man emerged from the car and hurried towards her.

'A damsel in distress to be sure...My God, what are you doing out on such a night?' She jerked her thumb backwards in the direction of her wrecked car.

'Dew, dew,' he said – 'Looks like you need 'elp! 'Op in.,' Despite her discomfort, Tanya grinned at his choice of words. 'You're in luck, Miss?' 'Tanya,' she obliged. '...I 'appen to be a male nurse. My 'ouse is just around the next corner. I'll soon sort you out!' he said. Without a thought for her safety at first...Tanya hopped awkwardly towards the car and got in. Once settled and the car had gathered speed, she cast a covert glance at the driver. He was easy on the eye, dark-haired – very Celtic – fortyish, quite a handsome profile in fact...but then so was Ted Bundy, the American murderer...She fidgetted in her seat and felt her heart beating faster. The fact that Bundy was charming and seemingly harmless also flitted through her memory. And didn't he torture his victims before he killed them?! She visibly jumped when the man next spoke.

'You're shivering…' he said, with a sideways look. 'The sooner you get out of those wet clothes, the better…' She gave him a weak smile, and swallowed hard.

Before long - he lived about a mile from where he had stopped – 'Tom', as he had quickly introduced himself, drove the car down a dirt lane leading to a small, quite isolated, cottage. Noting this, Tanya's imagination ran rampant. Her inner voice was insistently telling her to 'Calm down, stop jumping to conclusions. He seems like a nice guy…' 'Yes, just like Ted Bundy,' she replied The car stopped. Tom turned off the engine and turned to her:

'Can you manage to walk to the front door, or shall I carry you?' Flustered, she tried sounding calm… 'No thanks, I can hobble.'

'Righto,' he replied and opened the front door wider for her. She painfully followed him down the narrow hallway into a surprisingly bright living room ('Did you expect a torture chamber?' her inner voice asked. She quickly shut her up.) Switching on an electric fire, Tom turned and said:

'Look, I know this must be difficult for you - with me being a stranger an' all – but you can trust me. My sister lived 'yer with me, until recently, 'an there's some of 'er clothes still in the wardrobe. Why don' you take a shower – the water's still 'ot, an' then I'll look at that ankle.'

Tanya's other voice was babbling away about 'Psycho,' and she ignored her with some difficulty. Having locked the door, and safely showered, she calmed down a little. Having edited so many crime stories can, at times, be detrimental she thought. She felt weird putting on someone else's clothes – they just about fitted her - and wondered where Tom's sister was. Panicking, she suddenly thought of her own parents, worrying about her non-arrival; she'd have to use Tom's phone immediately. Aware too that her ankle was swelling alarmingly, and that the pain was increasing, she called out to Tom for assistance.

'Well,' he said, 'Don' you look the cat's whiskers in my sister's dress! I think I'll 'ave to put on my medical 'at now and take a look at that ankle.!'

'Sod my ankle…I need to phone my parents!' Tanya's nerves were jangling.

'That'll be easier said than done, Miss!' Irritated, she asked 'Why?'

'The phones around 'ere are all useless because of the storm. Now, sit you down an' I'll see what I can do for you!'

'Bloody hell! What a mess I've got myself into!' she gave an outsized sigh.

'No good frettin' Tanya…Try relaxin'…'He gave her a smile, which she interpreted as a leer, then gently bathed her ankle alternately in cold and hot water, dried it, and placed her leg on a leather pouffe.

'Now, keep your foot up on that and I'll make us a nice cup of tea. Would you like a sandwich?

'Ham or cheese? You must be starvin'!' Despite reservations, she said a weak 'Ham, thanks.'

Another, even more serious, dialogue started with her inner voice the moment he left for the kitchen.

'Supposing he puts poison in the tea or food? I'd be done for!' she told herself.

'Don't be so suspicious! He's no murderer…' it replied.

'How do you know? No-one knows I'm here, or where I am…' she said, biting a digit in between the words.

'Well, you'll just have to hope for the best, won't you!' it said. Tanya jumped as Tom shouted, 'Mustard with your 'am, Tanya?' She sniffed; he was very free with the Tanyas! Trying to lull her into a false sense of security, maybe? 'None, thanks,' she managed. Minutes later, he arrived in the room with a tray, noticed that Tanya was massaging her neck and put the tray on the coffee table.

'A touch of whiplash I think. I'll get you a neck brace.' This he did, which made her more comfortable, while nervously so. He then bade her eat her sandwich and drink her tea.

'Is your foot feelin' any better, gel?' he asked. She thought he was getting over familiar…' Drink up – don't want it to get cold,' he added. Despite his apparent kindness, doubts floated around like black confetti at a wedding. When she had finished the refreshments – with no ill effects, she realised with relief - Tom took away the china, and said almost as an aside as he was leaving the room, 'You'll have to stay the night, of course! You can sleep in Amanda's room.' The panic, which was on a see-saw, returned. But, what else could she do? The wind had died down, but the rain had gathered momentum and was pounding at the windows as if keen to gain entry. Even if she could walk okay – which she couldn't - she would get soaked to the skin. It was a no no situation!

After Tom had left the room, she gave it a more thorough search with her eyes. It was innocuous enough; fairly masculine in colour, furniture and design – more minimalist than 'cottagey,' although there were a few chinzy cushions and a pretty feminine jug on the dresser which didn't fit in. Once Tom's mother's perhaps, or his missing sister's? At that moment, Tanya's eyes took in a trunk-sized object, covered with a tartan rug in a corner of the room.

She didn't exactly know why she felt uncomfortable at finding it, but she did.

'So, do you think it contains a body then?' her inner voce teased.

'Of course not!' she replied hotly, while further assuring herself.

'He tended to my ankle and neck, he's fed and watered me, and offered me a bed for the night. For goodness sake, Tanya, stop being so paranoid.' Even so, despite her self-assurance, she felt compelled to look inside the chest. What was that about curiosity …Limping towards it, she sat down on a foot-stool, removed the rug, and as quietly as she could, lifted the lid a fraction. It creaked a little, which made her wince. She paused, expecting Tom to appear. He didn't. Opening the lid wider, the first thing which met her gaze was a dense black satin cape. She carefully removed it. What she found underneath made her place a hand over her mouth to stifle a gasp. There lay a snake-like whip, a black mask, a pair of silver handcuffs, and a rope, on top of what looked to be a black rubber cat-suit. Trembling, she put the cape back, closed the lid, and covered the chest. Almost speechless, she managed a weak 'Jesus!' What was his plan? Was he waiting until she was completely asleep and helpless? Her mouth felt dry and her thoughts scrambled. There was no inner voice to reassure her this time; her complete mental ability had shut down. Tanya almost fell into an armchair: 'Dew, dew.' she said. Gazing into space, it was a full five minutes before she recovered her equilibrium. Having switched off the electric light and the fire, and guided by a shaft of moonlight cast across the carpet of the second bedroom, she moved a small chest of drawers – slowly and with much effort - in front of the door. Then, still fully dressed, she got into bed. Sleep was impossible, for quite apart from being on 'red alert' listening for Tom's approach, an owl hooted, and a branch of a tree tapped on the window in the wind making her heartbeat go into overdrive. The clock was ticking inordinately loudly, and Tanya could hardly wait for the morning to come, when that irritating inner voice said:

'That's IF it comes…'

Somehow or other, sheer exhaustion then took over, and sleep came just before dawn. A loud knocking at the door jolted Tanya from slumber and she uttered a bemused: 'Who's there?' almost immediately realising that it could only be Tom.

'I can't seem to open the door…' he said, continuing after a pause…'I've brought you tea and toast.' Fully-fledged guilt overcame her; where was the trust one was supposed to have for humanity?! With humility coursing through every corpuscle, she hopped to the door, and huffing and puffing, moved the offending chest and opened the bedroom door. Facing her was the most incongruous sight she had ever seen. Her mouth dropped open.

'Mornin' Tanya. Breakfast is served…' he said with an evil smile. 'I heard you open my trunk last night…'

Sheer relief turned in a nano-second to panic.

'Meet 'The Man in Black, Mystic and Conjuror.' ' Tom roared with laughter, while it took several seconds for Tanya to recover from seeing him thus dressed. He went on:

'Before I studied medicine, I worked in a travelling circus with my sister Amanda. She's an acrobat and is appearing in Blackpool as we speak.' Putting down the tray, he left the room – only to return carrying a rope and a pair of handcuffs. Tanya could hardly breathe.

'Would you like me to show you one of my tricks now, Tanya? Of course, I'll need your assistance.'

Tanya and Justin had a candlelit Christmas wedding and Tom was guest of honour.

THE TWO SISTERS' CHARITY
Joy Lennick

Nadine, feeling marginally marinated in pungent Tandori chicken spices; her ears assailed by some sort of Punjabi lament - made a moue while fumbling in her purse for her door key as she reached the gate of her minute front garden. Garden being a more than kind description of the muddy-earthed strip and wind-blown single rose bush, its blooms long gone. More than evident too…was the rhythmic beating of what sounded like tom toms coming from the open windows of the lilac and lemon painted house opposite her temporary home. 'Oh, to be in England…' she thought as she opened the front door. Despite being American, a rendering of an imagined 'Greensleeves' playing somewhere over her head, made her grin. Not exactly to her taste, which was hardly refined, but still…Nadine was out of kilter – her partner Estelle had been a tad off-hand of late – or was the menopause responsible for her own mood swings, she wondered. She was getting edgy, nervous. Perhaps it was time they moved on.

Closing the abused door, Nadine shouted 'Hi Stell!' down the hallway, limping in the direction of what passed for their living room, for they ate and spent most of their home time there, mostly ignoring the dining room – using it to store accumulated junk, plus a good supply of candles, purchased at a bargain price. There was no answer to Nadine's greeting, which caused a frown. She found Estelle seated at the table counting five, ten and twenty pound notes and putting them into neat piles before securing them with elastic bands; plus a pile of pound coins. Her partner put a finger to her lips, so Nadine had no choice but to wait until she had finished counting; her face lightening as she asked 'How'd we do today?' Estelle turned towards her – 'We took two hundred and ninety- nine pounds! How'd you like them rosy apples?' They high-fived and Nadine felt a fleeting glow of satisfaction. 'The Lord be praised, hallelujah,' she said, pressing her hands together in prayer-like mode, noticing a brown stain on the ceiling as she gazed upwards. 'I'm getting peed off with this dump we blithely call home, Est. Let's split…Go somewhere a bit God-damned warmer. I didn't believe that 'four seasons in a day' crap, but it's true!' Nadine eased her bulky body into a scruffy grey velveteen armchair with a sigh. (Her size was genetic, her mother hardly a 'greyhound' when it came to comparisons, although Nadine's calorific intake was a factor.) 'Let's not make a hasty decision, Nad. The gravy's not bad here and the night life's great…' Estelle replied, adding the coins before her into a half-filled tin, which made a pleasing rattle when righted, while Nadine, rising from her chair, gave another sigh. Moving closer to her partner, she thrust out her arms and held her firmly by her shoulders, and licking her lips lasciviously, tried thrusting her tongue in her mouth. 'How about some wild time, Est…' she almost pleaded. 'Not now Nad – I have to meet Sid at The Three Grapes in half an hour!' She pushed Nadine away. 'Spoilsport! What's wrong with you lately?' If Estelle had heard her last remark, she wasn't letting on, and after putting the money in a bag and passing it to Nadine, she left the room to shower and change clothes.

Nadine half-filled the kettle with water, switched it on, and got busy with the ground coffee and cafetiere in Estelle's absence, mulling over her options as to the evening's entertainment. Discounting watching the television, she supposed she could tag along with Estelle, quickly dismissing the idea, only too aware that her partner liked to work alone on what she regarded as her input to the business. For it was a business, while a strange one... Nadine liked to sweeten her conscience – miniscule that it was - by giving 'reasonable' sums of money to deserving causes. It was also vital to keep nosey parkers from delving too deep. Occasionally, with much regret, when the takings were generous, they gave sizeable chunks of money to various charities, necessary to gain publicity, keep doubters off the scent and earn a veneer of respectability. Having poured her drink, she took two doughnuts from the cake tin, scoffing them with evident pleasure - licking the spilt jam noisily off her fingers while telling herself, yet again, that she'd start her diet the following day. Reflecting on the day's takings, her mood – assisted by the sugar intake – lifted a little. Life wasn't so bad. The prayer meeting and buffet lunch in The People's Hall in Ilford had gone well. Very well. And if Estelle played Sid right, maybe he'd let them use the recreation hall he owned in Essex for free!

Forty-nine years earlier, in a run-down street in a suburb of Chicago, U.S. of A., Elvira Dora Walters was screaming: 'Let me die. Please let me die...' like a banshee, in the last stages of labour. She gave birth to a 13lb daughter whom she called Nadia, vowing to never again have another baby. A vow that she kept. Despite the difficult delivery, Elvira – after a bout of cursing - forgave her only child and thereafter, suffering much hardship in the process (being an unmarried mother from the wrong side of the tracks), gave her daughter the best upbringing that she could afford. In fact, everything that she had never had, especially love, having been an abused child from a broken marriage. In return, Nadia became an over-indulged, crafty, rebellious, deviously clever… daughter. From an early age, she knew how to 'play' her mother with pretensions of affection and supposedly good behaviour. Although healthy in every other respect, one of Nadine's legs had been malformed from birth, leaving her with a pronounced limp - yet another reason for Elvira to pour honeyed love on to her only daughter. As she grew older, her increased tantrums were put down to boredom and 'Being too intelligent!' When Nadia's first teacher said to Elvira: 'I regret to have to inform you that Nadia wilfully cut off Sue Ellen's plaits this morning,' she refused to believe her, despite Sue Ellen tearfully confirming the fact. Other unpleasant incidents followed, and by the age of ten, Elvira's 'darling daughter' was smoking behind the school play-shed, playing truant, stealing and occasionally causing disruptions in the classroom by her bad behaviour. Elvira continued to go through life with veiled eyes, refusing to let herself believe that the only human being that she had ever loved could somehow be flawed.

Secure in her mother's love, Nadia knew how to manipulate and cajole when necessary, until one unforgettable day just after her sixteenth birthday. Returning from a shopping trip via an alleyway which led to her modest house, Elvira came across her daughter tussling with a male friend of Nadia's called Ned and witnessed a scene that would remain seared in her memory until her dying day. Although what happened next, happened in a second's blinding flash of sun against steel, Elvira – a hand clamped over her mouth in horror, spilled shopping around her, saw her daughter pull a knife from a deep pocket and plunge it into Ned's body. 'Oh, Nadia. What have you done?' she screamed, the blood seeming to drain from her own body as she ran forward and cradled Ned's head in her lap. He was still breathing but bleeding profusely from a wound in the side of his stomach. Ned's angel must have been on high alert as, in answer to Elvira's yells for help, a young man– an intern – out jogging, came rushing forward. After an understood, silent mime, Elvira tore off her white blouse and handed it to him. Reassuring the wounded lad, he pressed the garment and his hand firmly over the wound slowing the blood flow a little. Luckily there was a pay-phone on the corner, so Elvira was able to ring the local hospital, and Ned lived to try his luck with a more willing, less dangerous young woman. To Elvira's eternal torment, Nadia disappeared from her life forever on that same, indelible afternoon, and Elvira died 'From a heart attack' twelve months later – a prognosis her only friend disagreed with. Despite a police search continuing for Nadia for several years, she was never found.

During the 'limbo' years, as Nadia later referred to them, she changed her appearance and her name to Nadine Woodstock (oddly clinging to four letters of her first name like a comfort cloth). Doing whatever was necessary to survive, put her firmly on the wrong side of the tracks her mother had tried so desperately to escape from. By the time she was twenty, Nadine – auburn-haired and not unattractive - had 'shacked up' with numerous men and one woman, until she met Estelle that is. A natural blonde, lissome and with arresting facial features and green eyes, Nadine called her 'cat-like' and immediately felt that she had met her soul-mate, telling her: 'You're the one, Est. You must stay with me forever.' For her part, Estelle: a 'bad seed' from a wealthy family, found Nadine exciting and different, although she had no intention of staying faithful. Like Nadine, she knew 'all the tricks of the trade' – that trade involving fleecing money from unsuspecting folk whenever the opportunity arose. Bored, and with Nadine in particular drawn to religion – although Devil worship would have been more appropriate - the pair hatched a scheme whereby they could live quite comfortably 'In the name of Jesus.' Which was ironic in the circumstances. Neither saw any discrepancy in their thinking...

With money saved, the pair eventually flew to the UK and drew up a plan which would take them across Wales and England. Staying in cheap B & B's and frequenting local churches and trawling hospitals... was the first step; ascertaining who was 'On the way out...'' as Estelle succinctly put it, the second. Calling themselves 'The Two Sisters' Charity', they visited the frail and sick, and sometimes, if the patient died, depending on the circumstances, set up prayer meetings 'For the peace of the departed soul,' cleverly providing refreshments and even having raffles 'For the bereaved and charity' drawing in a respectful, respectable crowd. They became adept at their deception – even scanning the local papers for reports of accidents and illness; perhaps, in their twisted minds, convincing themselves of their goodness... As for their acting ability, they should have received an Oscar apiece. The fact that for every pound they made for charity, they kept at the very least two for themselves, they thought quite fair. They, after all, had expenses; had to live...

As time passed, the twosome grew even more ambitious and Nadine realised to her delight that, with her American twang, 'motherly figure' and reassuring voice, she had a strange hold on many people, while 'believers' willingly danced to her tune. The manipulative ways she had garnered when dealing with her mother, stood her in good stead. They organised tombolas and 'Walks for Charity,' and with gathering notoriety, the coffers grew fat. Folk singing was also embraced; dances held for cancer research, and many praised their efforts unreservedly. One Christmas, they went the whole hog and organised a special dinner with tree and personal gifts: local shops being generous in the extreme. Candles were lit and prayers said for the sick and departed: 'May God bless you''s filling the air. Financially, that year, several charities did fairly well, while 'their' charity did handsomely. In a quiet moment, Nadine recalled high-fiving Estelle after visiting a solicitor's office and being told that a 'Mrs. Edith Lilian Potter' – a dying woman the pair had befriended – '... has left you the sum of three thousand pounds.' They spent a wild weekend in Paris after that windfall, eschewing their usual modest garb and buying themselves more colourful, and in Estelle's case, quite outlandish clothes. It wasn't their only 'inheritance.' Having stayed in Darlington for a few months, they had befriended an ailing, aged bachelor called Joe Harborough, who – when he 'Kicked the bucket,' as Estelle termed death - bequeathed them five thousand pounds in his will 'To further promote the good work these fine women do.' On that occasion, they gave one thousand pounds to charity, thereby gaining themselves handy publicity and more kudos. As for paying taxes…as Estelle put it: 'Only fools pay taxes.'

Back to the present…

Awakening with a start, Nadine yawned, and bleary-eyed, checked her wrist-watch as Estelle sasheyed dramatically and noisily into the room. Staggering over to her partner's sprawled body, she stuck a teasing tongue in her nearest ear, retreating when Nadine attempted to caress her.

'Had a f.fun evening, Nad?' she guffawed loudly, turned off the TV and fell into a nearby chair.

'You're drunk again, Stell. Hardly one of Jesus' ideal little helpers are you?'

'Sod Jesus!' said Estelle, taking off her junk jewellery and throwing it on the table with a clatter.

'Cool! Oh, very cool! Carry on like that, and you'll soon find that 'being detained at her Majesty's pleasure' doesn't mean dining in Buck House!' Estelle made a gesture that was blatantly un-polite.

'Have you quite fin…fish…finished, MOM!' Estelle slurred, finding it difficult to control her tongue or focus properly.

'You stupid bitch! I'll talk to you in the morning,

headache or not…' Exit Nadine, orchestrated by a slammed door.

A week later – on a Friday – the two women were conducting 'A Tea For Tom' meeting in an idyllic hamlet venue near the village of Blackmore in Essex: a building owned by the aforementioned Sid of 'The Three Grapes.' Both Nadine and Estelle were soberly dressed in black trousers and high-necked white blouses topped by sensible cardigans against the winter chill. Estelle, with a pout, preferring the leopard-print mini skirt, scarlet silk top and blonde wig she wore in private, and when she did occasional pub bar work in between their 'calling work.'

'Where would you like me to put this Victoria sponge, Ms. Woodstock?' A whey-faced, scrawny woman they knew to be Sid's sister smiled nervously.

'Oh, what a darling you are, Sarah, especially after making all those cheese and cucumber   sandwiches and those yummy butterfly cakes. Bless you!' Sarah blushed. Another 'upright   and   kindly   citizen' introduced as a Mrs Spalding, hovered in the background, loaded with goodies she too had made. There seemed to be a stream of people willing to help, mindful of the terrible accident that had befallen the young son of a member of the church: Tom Burrows, local paper-boy, aged fifteen. The winding country lanes were dangerous, and a speeding motorist had taken Mr. and Mrs. Burrows only son from them in a few mad and horrendous seconds. Nadine cleared her throat:

'Ladies and gentlemen…' she paused and placed one hand over her heart to great effect,

'We all know why we are gathered here today – although only the good Lord really knows why it should be so…John and Kathy Burrows' only son has been taken to live with Jesus. He was only fifteen, with all his life before him but he is now at peace. My sister, Estelle, will be collecting for Tom's parents, and we will also be giving a small donation to charity. Thank you for your support and caring. God bless you all.'

The hall was packed and everyone clapped enthusiastically. There were many wet cheeks and John and Kathy Burrows thanked Nadine with fervour while she hugged them. Candles were lit and the passed bucket was half-filled within the shortest time. After the gathering had sung another hymn and the last of the food had been consumed, John Burrows approached Nadine again.

'I've lost two members of my family to cancer, Nadine, so we won't keep the money collected for us. Please take it and give it all for research.''

Nadine was visibly moved and the meeting came to a close. Within three days, 'the sisters' had high-tailed it to Spain.

'Bless you all!' words familiar to Nadine's tongue, rang around a café in Estepona, Southern Spain. Another 'charity gathering;' 'more suckers' Estelle thought – about as religious as a solipsist.

A year had passed pleasantly by, and the two women, lapping up the continental life and the watery, winter sunshine, were relaxing on the patio of their rented apartment. Rising from her lounger, Estelle said that she was 'Off to buy some Vodka! Won't be long, hon.' Eyes closed, Nadine was musing on the past, half listening to the gentle caressing sound of the

Mediterranian waves on the sandy shore-line nearby; mindful of a gentle breeze on her bare arms. Glancing at the calendar on the wall through the window, she sniggered.

'Here we are in the midst of the Winter Solstice…' she said out loud, 'I wonder what the temperature is in the UK?'

Eyes downcast, idly watching an insect, Nadine was suddenly aware of a shadowy presence and visibly jumped as a man appeared.

'Hello, Nadine – surprise, surprise! I bet you didn't expect to see me again…How are your caring soirees going? I must say, you're looking very prosperous…' the man cast a glance at Nadine's new gold watch and necklace.

'Did you really think that the good sisters scam would go on forever?' He continued.

For once in her life, Nadine's words seemed cemented in her mouth.

'May I?' the man eased himself into a cane chair opposite her.

'It's amazing how small a world it is and how coincidence plays such a mysterious part in   all our lives. I was playing bowls one day, and got chatting to a top bowler who travels the UK.

He'd lost his mother to cancer the year before, and mentioned a couple of women who had prayed for her soul, collecting a huge amount of money for charity in the process.'

Nadine opened her mouth to speak but only a squeak emerged. She squirmed in her seat, and was visibly perspiring to excess. The man continued:

'Suspicious that the women were insincere –I'd

have called them 'scavengers'…'' the man stopped talking for a long moment to let his words sink in, while Nadine looked about ready to combust -   '…he started asking a few questions, contacted the appropriate charity, and was dismayed to discover that only a quarter of the money raised was handed over. That led me thinking, Nadine…So I did the same. Most of the major charities keep excellent records by the way…' By this time, the colour in Nadine's cheeks had heightened and she started wiping her hands on her trousers.

'I listened to your familiar clap-trap in the café the other day, Nadine. Fancy my wife and I choosing to have a late holiday in Estepona! Do you know, it is over a year since our Tom was killed? After I did a bit of detective work, I found out that you and your 'sister' are nothing but a pair of charlatans who prey on the bereaved and grieving. I have nothing but contempt for you.'

Fumbling in his pocket, John Burrows pulled out a small hand gun fixed with a silencer, and fired two blanks at Nadine's body. Naturally, the look on her face was one of horror, and her body instinctively jerked backwards. John left the scene without a backward glance, satisfied that he had put the fear of God into her. What he didn't know was that when Estelle later found her, she was dead. Shocked and grief- stricken, Estelle drank the whole bottle of vodka she had just bought. As she already had enough alcohol in her system to make her ill, further fuelled by an ecstasy tablet, the vodka tipped her over the edge.

A colleague of Estelle's found their two bodies – and their small, motley band of friends was, understandably shocked, as was John Burrows when he heard. It would be a bare-faced lie to say that he grieved for either woman, and he felt a small measure of satisfaction when he heard that every euro of the collection made in their memory went to an appropriate charity.

'OLD RED' AND HIS RED HERRING
KJ Rollinson

My husband, Peter, and I joined his uncle for a drink in the Tredegar Arms Pub, where traditionally the local Hunt gathered prior to the Boxing Day meet. Peter's uncle for many years in the past had been the master of the hounds of the Hunt. I was wearing my new white coat, a Christmas present from Peter, together with a matching red hat, scarf and gloves. I was not at all appreciative that my nose was beginning to match the colour of my accessories as I stamped my feet to keep warm I was very glad when Uncle Jimmy suggested that because the horses and hounds had not yet arrived we retreat into the cosy warmth of the pub to escape from the cold biting wind.

It was a traditional 'oldy worldy' pub, with dark low beams, and a crackling apple log fire. It was suitably decorated to proclaim the festive season and Uncle Jimmy and I managed to get a table in a corner while Peter went up to the bar for our drinks.

When he returned Uncle Jimmy started to reminisce about past Meets. This was the time before Anti-blood sports and I must admit that for most people the Boxing Day Meet was just a morning out to witness a colourful spectacle with some of the hunt members in hunting pink and the friendly excited hounds, without much thought given to the fate of the poor fox.

I am not sure how - but our conversation turned to the training of young scent hounds. My husband's uncle disputed the old story that a pungent kipper – known as a red herring – would be dragged along a trail until a puppy learned to follow the scent. Later when the dog was being trained to follow the odour of a fox or badger, the trainer would drag a red herring perpendicular to the animal's trail to confuse the hound. Thus it would eventually learn to follow the correct scent.

'Tell Kath about that dog fox the Hunt encountered a few years back,' Peter said to Uncle Jimmy. 'He planted a 'red herring didn't he?'

Uncle Jimmy snorted and banged his half empty pint glass on to the table. 'My God, you mean the wily fox we called Old Red? Yeah, we came a right cropper when he played his trick on us.'

'What a fox intentionally misled you?' I said with some disbelieve.

'Yes, Old Red knew what he was doing that's for sure,' Uncle Jimmy replied. 'I don't mean he said to himself 'right I'm, going to plant a 'red herring', but he very definitely led us on a false trail and distracted us on purpose to cause our downfall.'

I was now intrigued, 'Have you got time to tell the story before the Hunt arrives?'

Peter glanced at his watch. 'We've got plenty of time before they get here; please tell us Uncle Jimmy.'

'Yes, OK - though you've heard it before Peter.'

I know I have - but I never tire of listening to it.'

Uncle Jimmy took another sip of his pint, wiped his mouth and started his tale.

'The Hunt had tried for several years to catch Old Red but he always eluded us. This time our hounds got his scent early as we sped across open fields. We galloped after him and he led us uphill. I swear the little beggar kept on turning his head to make sure we were following him. It was January, the time when

49

foxes are very territorial because it's their mating season, and I thought he would probably be loathe to stray outside his own boundary, which would make our task that much easier to catch him. Uncle Jimmy gave a rueful laugh, 'In hindsight I realised that he knew his own area very well indeed. Anyway, let's got on with the story.

As I said we were galloping up this hill, and by standing in my stirrups I could just see over the brow. In the near distance I observed that Old Red had sat down, his tongue lolling out from the side of his mouth, as if he was too exhausted to go any further.

I twisted in my saddle and shouted back to the rest of the Hunt, 'We've got him now. He's tiring.' The huntsman blew his horn and I, and the pack of hounds, raced forward excitedly.

As I got to the top of the hill I saw a wide open ditch in front of me. My horse cleared it easily, together with most of the hounds, but to my horror I found we all landed in deep squelching mud, which lay concealed in a hollow. Fortunately, the other riders, hearing the commotion of the howling, panicking hounds, reigned to a halt at the brow of the hill, or tentatively picked their way down the side of the ditch and skirted the quagmire and thus avoided the predicament that I had landed in.

Eventually we all managed to free ourselves from the sucking mud and what a bedraggled lot we looked. My pink hunting jacket was now a dirty brown, and you know what dogs are – they will insist on standing next to people to shake themselves. Well, by the time they'd finished spraying everybody most of the riders were covered in mud splashes. When order was at last restored it was decided to abandon the Hunt.' Uncle Jimmy laughed. 'In any case there was no sign of the fox by this time, because I'd seen Old Red nonchalantly trot off to safety once he had seen his ploy had worked.'

Uncle Jimmy put his empty pint glass down on the table. 'Peter! My God! I've just realised you've planted a red herring haven't you!? I swear you asked me to tell that tale to intentionally distract me from having another pint.' Uncle Jimmy waved an accusing finger at my husband.

Peter and I laughed. 'Come on,' Peter said, 'I can hear the Hunt arriving.'

THE END OF THE WORLD
KJ Rollinson

I opened my lounge curtains and stared through the window of my high rise flat. My mind half registered the distant trees across the park; dark against dark, silent silhouettes against the night sky, with street and house lights twinkling through the bare branches as if they were competing with the stars which shone brightly in a cloudless sky.

Usually when I looked out through the window from my elevated position I felt safe, cocooned in my isolation, but not tonight. Tonight as I looked up at the night sky I was full of foreboding. I felt lonely, apprehensive. I gazed at the stars, I searched infinity, as if this intense preoccupation should provide me with the answers to what was troubling me.

I raised my brandy glass to my lips, found it was empty, and weaved to the sideboard to pour myself another drink. I had been drinking steadily for the last hour. I had lost count of the number I had consumed after the fourth.

I concentrated on pouring the drink into the glass, and not onto the floor, and I murmured 'the moving hand moves on and having drunk,' – I hiccupped and raised my glass to my reflection which gazed back at me blurrily from the mirror hanging above the sideboard. I mentally apologised to Omar Khayyam, and wondered whether he, as an astronomer as well as a poet, would have had any thoughts on what was supposed to happen

I had read my Horoscope in the local paper – 'make no decisions in December you will regret'. I had flicked to the Horoscope page of a magazine – 'in the month of December you are in for a big surprise. A few days before the festive season you will find a solution to all that is worrying you.' Bloody vague as usual I thought. I always start swearing when I have had too much to drink. Not surprising really under the circumstances. I was in a dithering dilemma about yet another prediction that the world was going to end. This time it was supposed to happen on the 21st December, 2012. It was now ten minutes to midnight on the 20th December.

I had been on the internet for weeks reading about this latest Armageddon scenario and gleaned all the information about previous predictions. I had absorbed all the warnings of Nostradamus, Nassa, the Mayan Calendar, Merlin, Mother Shipton, even bloody Britney Spears had got in on the act on this occasion.

I had bought the 'The Survival Guide' on 'How to survive December 21st, 2012, and read other people's comments on their blogs. One bright spark had suggested that as only half of the world would be devastated, and he thought with Africa faring the best, it would be good idea to buy real estate there and make a killing!

Part of me kept on saying that despite global warnings, threats of meteorites, asteroids colliding with the earth and wiping us out, not to mention hurricanes, tornadoes and tsunamis, the 'big bang' or whatever, was not going to happen. Why then did I have this strong premonition that something was going to happen on the 21st December?

Why was I sat here in my flat, all on my own, getting pissed? Why hadn't I bought any Christmas pressies, crackers, or Christmas cards? I knew the answer – because I couldn't seem to get it out of mind that whatever I did would be a sheer waste of time.

In an endeavour to cheer myself up I started to think of all the advantages of the world ending. I put my glass down on a nearby coffee table, and brought my hands close to my face – why did I seem to have twenty fingers? I shook my head vigorously, and was relieved when I found my fingers returned to their normal number. I started to count off the number of advantages to me if the demise of the world was to happen. No.1. I wouldn't have to complete my tax return. No.2. I wouldn't have to get my bunions done. No.3. I wouldn't have to carry on paying my mortgage. No.4. I could forget about my diet. No.5. I wouldn't have to do any more housework. Not that I did much anyway as I paid a cleaner to do it. Ah yes, No.6. I wouldn't have to pay the cleaner. No.7. I could forget about my boring office job. My fingers again blurred into double digits so I gave up counting - anyway it wasn't all bad!

I weaved back over to the sideboard for another brandy; saw that the bottle was empty so poured a whisky instead. I squinted at my watch, almost midnight, and I wondered whether the end of the world would happen at one minute past twelve or whether it would leave me in suspense and wait to the very last second of the 21st.For goodness sake! Pull yourself together I told myself angrily, nothing is going to happen!

I staggered to the window and looked (somewhat in a blur) at the peaceful scene outside. I breathed deeply and started to convince myself I was perfectly safe in my high-rise heaven as I listened to the muted soothing traffic sounds. I began to relax. I inhaled deeply again. The man in the moon gazed down seemingly bemused as I swayed back and forth. I heard the clock in the hall announce the midnight hour. Perhaps I would turn into a pumpkin, I thought and then I needn't worry about ruddy 21st December!

I wiped away the perspiration from my brow, God! I needed fresh air. I was starting to feel somewhat queasy. I wrestled with the window cord. The window was one of those old fashioned sash cord things and it was stuck. I rattled the window frame in exasperation and scrambled on to the windowsill and jiggled with the cord. The blasted thing - nothing moved. In exasperation I pushed my shoulder with all my strength against the top half of the window.

Suddenly, without warning, the window crashed down. I overbalanced. I put my hand out to steady myself, caught hold of the rotting wood frame which disintegrated and crumbled beneath my clutching fingers, and I found myself falling 100ft. towards the spiked railings which bordered the flats.

I just had time to think at least I do not have to worry about the 'big bang!'

THE LAST BET
KJ Rollinson

Al Hartland eased himself into the driving seat, turned on the engine and windscreen wipers, and drove the car slowly out of the pub cark park.

'Let's hope this lot will have stopped by the morning,' he said as he leaned forward, peered anxiously through the car window and watched the driving rain.

His passenger, Bob Wild shook his head. 'Relax mate. It won't matter much anyway. It should mean there'll be less people around at the stables, when you arrive. The lads won't be exercising many 'orses if this keeps up. The ground will be too soft.'

Hartland grunted. 'That's true, but it might make it difficult for me to get up the back lane to the stables, if it's still raining cats and dogs, and I can hardly go up the front drive, can I? I mean I don't want to advertise the fact that a strange car towing a horse van has arrived to pinch one of the most famous horse in history,' he said scathingly.

'Why on earth did you plan to pinch the horse at this time of the year, anyway?' Wild queried.

'That wasn't my decision,' came the reply. 'The client decided it should be now; something to do with his schedule wouldn't allow it to be later on in the year. Evidently this Arab has fingers in many pies. Are you sure you can get Sherpa into the horse box tomorrow?' Al Hartland asked anxiously.

'A piece of cake. Stop worrying will yer.' Wild answered with annoyance.

'Tell me again how you are going to do it. You

needn't look at me like that. I want to make sure your timing is perfect,' Al Hartland said firmly.

Wild sighed and answered with exaggerated slowness. 'At 9.30 a.m. I walk up to Tom Bates, and tell him our stables have had a phone call from Mr Brown, a famous local breeder, who has offered Sherpa's owner a large stud-fee. Unfortunately the mare he had in mind doesn't travel very well. Mr. Brown has arranged for Sherpa to cover the mare at their stables. I've to tell him that a horse box will arrive to collect Sherpa. I'll say he needn't stay as I can get Sherpa into the horse box on me own.'

Wild wiped the inside of his half of the windscreen with a gloved hand, and added, 'If anyone is going to get caught it'll be Bates. He's looked after Sherpa for months; so as soon as they realise the horse is missing they'll be on his tail, not ours. For good measure I've planted some doped sugar cubes. They know he's always giving Sherpa sugar. They're sure to find them, and suspicion will fall on him. There satisfied.'

Al Hartland looked at the weasel-faced countenance of his acquaintance in annoyance. The more he was in Wild's company the more he disliked him. He was too cocky and too young for this type of job. The sooner Al could return to London the better. He hated this place. Nothing but trees and fields everywhere, and it seemed to rain all the time up here in the North of England. Give him the streets of old London town anytime. He was used to dealing with professionals, not like this young upstart.

When he had been approached with the very tempting financial offer to kidnap the racehorse Sherpa for an Arab millionaire, the money on offer was more than his wildest dreams. Unfortunately he hadn't the right contacts, until he was put in touch with Bob Wild, who had lost a lot of money betting on horses, and was in debt up to his greasy neck. He worked at a stable where several owners kept their racehorses. One of these was Sherpa.

Sherpa had become a legend after winning every race he entered. Even the great Lester Piggott had ridden him and said of him, 'nothing fazes that horse. He made the race look easy.'

Sherpa's days of racing were now finished and he had been sold for stud purposes. His new owner had paid a phenomenal price for the race horse but considered it was worth it in view of Sherpa's impeccable pedigree and past winning form.

Bob Wild rubbed his hands. 'I can't wait to get my hands on the ten grand you're going to pay me. I'll get a new car with leopard covered seats, pay off the loan sharks, and get me a nice curvy blonde.'

'You won't,' Al replied sharply. 'Not the car anyway. And only pay off the sharks who are breathing down your neck the most. You don't want it broadcast that you've all of a sudden come into a lot of money.'

'Alright, keep yer hair on,' Bob Wild answered irritably. 'A man can dream can't he? Anyroad, I could easily say I'd been lucky on the 'orses, - had a big win, and that's why I was throwing me money around.'

'Just watch it that's all,' but the older man's tone was placatory. He realised he knew nothing about horses, and had to rely on Wild to get Sherpa into the horsebox.

Hartland stopped the car in a lay-by when they came to Folifoot, a small village a few miles from Harrogate, where the youth lived with his parents.

'Right I'll meet you at the stables at 9.30 sharp, with the horsebox. You're sure you'll have doped the horse sufficiently so that it won't be any trouble? I don't want to have to deal with a highly strung race horse kicking the sides of the box in, when I'm driving to Milford Haven. I wouldn't have a clue how to deal with the wretched animal.'

'How many more times do I have to tell you the 'orse will be quiet when you hand it over,' Wild said impatiently. 'When will you give me my money?'

'You'll get your money alright after I've checked the horse is OK.'

'Stop worrying, will yer. How many more times do I have to tell you I'll have given the 'orse just enough dope to make it very quiet for the journey. Why are you driving to Milford Haven? Isn't it some godforsaken place somewhere in Wales?'

Hartland looked at his accomplice in annoyance. 'That's exactly why a 'godforsaken' place has been chosen, you moron, so I don't attract attention. It has loads of oil tankers going in and out. This Arab bloke does business there. Has his own tanker, and is shipping the horse out that way.'

Wild shook his head and sniffed, 'I still think the time of the year is dodgy to be doing this. 'Ere have this in case you have holdups 'cos of the condition of the roads or something.' He slipped Al Hartland a syringe. 'Give him half of this should he start to get too lively.'

'Bloody hell!' Hartland exclaimed, as he looked aghast at the syringe, lying in his open palm. 'How the hell do you expect me to give him this? I told you I don't know nothing about flaming horses.'

'Strewth!' Wild said exasperatedly. 'You only have to shove it into sugar cubes if you don't fancy pushing it into the 'orse's arse. 'Here,' Wild rummaged in his raincoat pocket and withdrew three sugar lumps wrapped in paper. 'Insert the syringe through the paper into the cubes – now that's not hard is it? But make sure you only use half a syringe. You don't want to find you've a dead horse on your hands.'

Hartland looked dubiously at the cubes, and hurriedly returned them and the syringe to Wild. 'Give 'em to me tomorrow morning. My coat's wringing wet at the moment; I don't want to get the sugar damp, and I don't fancy carrying that syringe in a pocket. I might do meself an injury.'

Wild sniggered, 'You probably won't need 'em anyway. I just thought they'd be useful in case you're delayed.' He looked anxiously at the darkening sky. 'Looks like snow to me,' he wrapped his scarf inside his coat before climbing out of the car.

When the two men met the following morning they were relieved to find the rain had stopped. The sun's weak rays were peeping through a cloudy sky, valiantly trying to lighten the bitterly cold January day.

Al Hartland shivered and thrust his hands into his pockets. He nodded at the sky. 'Now it's stopped raining, will it mean there'll be more people at the stables?'

'I doubt it. The going will still be too soft for most of the horses.' Wild replied as he glanced at his watch, 'In any case those horses that don't mind soft ground will have gone out by now. He looked around, 'Where have you parked the box?'

Hartland indicated with his head. 'It's parked behind the stables. The less people see it, the better.'

'OK. You go back and get the ramp down and I'll get Sherpa,' Wild replied as he hurried towards the stables.

Hartland waited anxiously besides the lowered ramp, wondering what was taking his accomplice so long. Eventually Wild appeared leading a very docile looking horse. He looked triumphantly at Hartland. 'What did I tell yer, a piece of cake. I told Bates what was supposed to be 'appening, so he left me to it and cleared off to muck out a stable.' He patted Sherpa's neck, 'I've given him three sugars. I reckon he'll 'ave a snooze once he's in the box.' He led the horse up the ramp followed by Harland. Sherpa immediately lay down on his side and stretched out his legs.

'There, he'll be sleeping like a babe in a few minutes.' Wild turned to Hartland, held out a cupped palm and gesticulated with his fingers, 'Right give me my money now. My part in this caper is finished. '

Hartland produced a large bulging envelope. 'Open your coat then and I'll put it into your inside pocket.' Wild stepped closer to Hartland and did as he was bid.

Suddenly a flick-knife appeared in Hartland's hands and with expertise he plunged it into Wild's chest up to the hilt.

The injured man clutched at Hartland's coat. 'Why?' he gurgled. Blood splashed from his mouth.

Hartland easily removed Wild's hands from his coat and pushed him backwards. Wild crashed to the floor, and lay on his back staring up at his ruthless colleague.

Hartland shrugged. 'It's just that I didn't trust you. All your talk of blondes and cars. I know your type. You'd spend, spend, spend. No one would've believed you'd won the money on the gee-gees, you're a loser mate. I can't afford to take any chances, there's too much at stake.' He laughed, 'You've placed your last bet pal.' He bent down and pulled the knife from Wild's chest, and wiped the blade on the dying man's coat.

'Be still your wild beating heart,' he smiled grimly at his own macabre pun. Hartland looked down at Wild's body lying by the side of the horse. He kneeled beside Sherpa and tentatively patted his neck, and cocked an ear to listen to the snores issuing from the horse's nostrils. Satisfied that Sherpa would cause him no trouble he looked again at the prone form of Bob Wild and noticed he was still breathing.

'You won't be breathing for long, mate. Anway, you'll be feeding the fishes when I get to the coast.' He patted Wild's chest. 'In the meantime you can keep the horse company.' He rose and brushed the knees of his trousers and turned to exit the horse box.

'What the hell!' he said as he felt a sharp pain in his ankle. He whipped around when he heard a gurgling laugh and saw Wild, frothy blood spewing from his grinning mouth and holding up the empty syringe before it fell from his hand. The dying man, his remaining strength spent, collapsed on his back. Hartland kicked Wild viciously in the head before he staggered down the ramp, stumbled, and tried to crawl towards the car. He felt his limbs going numb and his brain telling him to sleep. He shook his head in an effort to clear it before he collapsed unconscious.

The sun had long given up its brave attempt to shine. The clouds had gathered in a thick layer and heavy snow was now falling. The few horses which had gone out returned from their practice gallop. One rider jumped down from his mount and hugged the sleeves of his polo-neck sweater.

'Brr. By God! It's turned cold.'

'Yes,' his colleague replied as he pulled a rug over his horse, 'I bet it's below freezing now. Come on. Let's get the horses in and have a cuppa.'

FOUND IN TRANSLATION
Maggie Chapman

What an enjoyable evening it had been. It was a long time since Kate had been out and really enjoyed herself. Just Josie, Alan, Peter and herself. There had been no references to either her or Peter being 'eligible', that they 'looked well together', or 'what a nice couple'. The only comment was 'we must do this again sometime,' and that was because they had all enjoyed themselves so much. As she drove home, Kate thought how relieved she was that Josie hadn't pushed Peter at her and they had established that it was just an evening catching up with friends and colleagues. She was tired of her other friends trying to play matchmaker.

When Kate returned home just before eleven, both the children were watching television, and she was about to say that it was time they were in bed, when she remembered that it was Friday, no school, and besides they weren't babies anymore. Alex was seventeen and Sandra was sixteen.

As she went upstairs to change, she thought how the time had flown. It had been physically and emotionally taxing to overcome the first two years after the separation from her husband. She didn't even have the satisfaction of being able to totally put the blame on him. He hadn't beaten her, or been unfaithful; they just didn't get on any more. It had all started when he had objected to the idea of her going back to teaching, although the extra money would have meant having a car each, and going on holiday, both of which had been forfeited when the children had come along seven years earlier.

She had ignored his argument about being at home for the children, being too rushed, who would pick the children up after school. She knew that there would be some difficulties, but was confident that she could cope, so she had gone ahead and started teaching again part-time. She had sorted childcare for the days she was unable to pick the children up from school and tried to carry on as normal. That was the beginning of the end. Argument after argument then he just left.

The children still saw their Dad Clive, every Sunday for years. Occasionally he took them on holiday. Any bitterness or resentment had long gone. He had remarried five years ago but the children still visited every Sunday The hard work was over and done with and Alex and Sandra, her children were good company now. She knew it would be short lived as they were already beginning to lead their own lives and Kate knew that it was only a matter of time before she would be on her own more and more. However at the moment they were very much with her.

As she walked back downstairs to make a hot drink she realised that she was at a point in her life when she was drifting. Friends were eager for her to have someone else in her life and she was kicking against it. Perhaps it was time for her to take a different approach.

'Anyone for a drink' Kate asked cheerfully.

'Oh! Mum, Sandra and I were just wondering. You haven't forgotten about the Spanish student who's coming tomorrow have you?' Alex said.

'That's not until next week'

'Mum you're impossible, it's tomorrow the first'

Kate took the diary out of her bag before she insisted. 'You're right Alex, why didn't you tell me before I went out, I'll have to go and clean the attic, it's such a mess up there. I know it's late, but could you give me a hand?'

'Can't it wait until tomorrow Mum?' complained Alex.

'Come on, we used to enjoy cleaning out the attic, remember how you always wanted to do it the pair of you?'

'That was years ago Mum.' Sandra piped in laughing at the memory. 'But okay. We'll do it, come on Alex, it is your student you know.'

'I'm not sure what I'm going to do with another seventeen year old, I hope you're going to entertain him Alex'

'I'll entertain him'' purred Sandra trying to display some feminine appeal.

Sandra, that's enough, I'm surprised at you. Alex, I'll hold you responsible for him and Sandra'

All three climbed the steep stairs to the third floor equipped with dusters, brushes and clean linen. It wasn't really such a bad room, the window was large, and held the sun the whole morning, so when he arrived it would look much brighter than it did now.

''I often thought of having this room for myself,' Kate said.

'You could hide all your men friends up here Mum and we wouldn't know anything about it.' Sandra said playfully.

'Sandra I don't believe my ears, that's the second remark you've made to me about having a man in my life. That's not like you. Please behave,' Kate said.

Kate saw Sandra and Alex exchange a brief glance, and Sandra shaking her head. So she said, 'Perhaps you've got something to say as well Alex, how many men friends do I have? I don't like to say this and I don't think I have before, but how many men friends do you think I could lure up here with two monsters like you around?'

Alex looked at his mother, held his breath for a moment and sighed resolutely before he spoke.

'How did tonight go Mum? Did Josie have someone lined up for you? We were talking about you having a night out. It's only a couple of years before we both leave, and well, you ought to have a man around the house.' Alex spoke with a serious tone n his voice Kate hadn't heard before and she was touched by his concern, but angry at his suggestion that she needed someone.

'A man! Don't you start, I've had enough of men being pushed at me left right and centre by my so called friends, without you two pushing me into the arms of every man I might meet. Just stop it. It's too late at night for this conversation.'

'That's the point Mum, it must be lonely for you, it's not easy for me to say this Mum, but recently I've realised how much a relationship can... well.... can be ... important.' Alex said sheepishly.

'Alex, I hope you don't mean what I think you mean, and if you do, don't tell me anymore. I can't believe it, and in front of Sandra.'

'Mum, you told me the facts of life at fourteen, and anyway Alex only means that you should start enjoying yourself, we don't want you to get married again.' Sandra said.

'Enough! Let's talk about something else. Tell me about this Spanish boy, what's his name.' Kate said dismissing the previous conversation, but the ideas suggested by her children of all people, were niggling in her mind. She wondered what conversations had taken place for these thoughts to have got into their heads in the first place

Alex removed the tension from the conversation, by pronouncing that his name was Manuel and he was a waiter. Kate joined in the frivolity and said in that case he was coming to the right place

The room was soon tidied and prepared and they all agreed they deserved a cup of coffee. It was half past twelve, but Kate was not easy in her mind about what had been said. They certainly were not children anymore; was she naive? Had she gone wrong somewhere? Should she discuss these things with her children? She decided to bring up the matter of relationships again, hers and theirs.

She carried the three cups in carefully, and placed them on the table. 'Well children, if I may be so bold, I'll ask you again what's on your collective minds? Has anyone put you up to this?'

'Mum just tell us, if you did get mar...., if you should ever consider having a relationship with someone else, what would he be like?'

'What a question. How do I know?'

'Oh Mum, just use your imagination' said Sandra, who was very good at using hers. 'Just think it's one of those games we used to play where you write down wishes on a piece of paper.'

'Okay. He'd be tall, clean, that's important, not particularly well dressed, not particularly handsome, dark, perhaps, friendly, with a nice smile, in armour on a white charger, to take me away from all this. How's that?'

'Well you're not difficult to please; there must be lots of people like that around.' said Alex sarcastically.

'Fair is fair Sandra, now you tell me your image of your ideal young man.'

'I'll tell you that tomorrow, when our Spanish student arrives.' said Sandra provocatively.

'You little minx, I don't like the tone of this conversation at all.' Kate said trying to be humorous.

'Oh Mum, you must admit, that the prospect of an attractive young Spaniard all to yourself is something of a novelty, not to mention exciting.'

'As long as you keep him occupied in proper activities, and not leave him hanging around me. I'll make him more than welcome. Anyway, I expect his parents have warned him against young ladies like you.' Let's go to bed, he'll be here at eleven. I suggest you both go down to the school early in the morning to pick him up.'

'He's coming with one of the Spanish school masters, the Professora I think, so if he can't speak English, he'll have an interpreter, though goodness knows where Proffesora; (is that right Alex), is going to stay; with one of our teachers I suppose.' Sandra informed her mum.

It was late when Kate woke the next morning. She waved Alex and Sandra off and said, 'don't hurry back I need some time to sort myself out.'

It had taken her a long time to go to sleep last night. She really didn't want an addition to the family for a month, but she mustn't think like that. Poor thing, it's probably his first time away from home, anyway he'll be at school with the children for the first two weeks, and then it's the half term break, thank goodness.

She busily made sandwiches so that she would have something to offer them to eat when they arrived, because it looked as though lunch was going to be very late. Kate, washed the breakfast dishes, dressed and prepared the salad to have with lunch and was just making herself a cup of coffee, when Sandra came in alone.

'Where's the new arrival, and Alex?' Asked Kate

'They're coming later; they have to sort out which boys are going to which family.'

'What's our boy like, does he live up to your expectations?'

'There are one or two attractive ones, but we don't know who we're having yet. Do you think I'm attractive Mum?'

'What a silly question. Of course I think so; you're beautiful. You are beautiful. You must believe that. You're Sandra, You're you. You're unique. Beauty's not the most important thing. You have to be a nice person and you're a nice person and that's far more important.'

I know, I'm not particularly good looking, but I've got a nice smile, like your Mr Wonderful.'

'You're my Miss Wonderful.' said Kate giving Sandra a hug.

'I want him to like me that's all.' Sandra said more cheerfully.

'He's sure to Sandra, now put on your best smile; I'll make you a drink.'

They cheered each other up over a cup of coffee. Sandra was facing the window and suddenly she jumped up, wiped her mouth with a tissue, pulled at her top over her slim waist to reach the top of her jeans and flicked her dark hair back. Then gave a wide smile as she said, 'I can hear them coming.'

Alex walked in first followed by a tall dark man, clearly over forty, smartly dressed in grey trousers, with a maroon sweater over his casual pink shirt. Fortunately he didn't see Sandra's look of disappointment as she forced a smile. He returned Sandra's smile and offered his hand.

'This is Gustavo, Mum. He's the tutor of the group, and he wondered if it would be alright if he could stay with us. The only thing is, he's come to stay for a year. I told him it would be alright, that you would be glad of the company.' Alex said as confidently as he could.

Kate and Sandra looked at each other in amazement, but neither spoke. Alex frowned as the silence became embarrassing. Kate was the first to sense the silence and broke it.

'Wherever are my manners, do come in Gustavo, please make yourself at home, it's just that we expected someone younger. Oh I don't mean that you're old, it's....it's,' Kate stumbled into silence again.

'Please. Please, Mrs...'

'Please call me Kate.'

'Ah, yes Kate, like 'Kiss me Kate' no?'

Both children laughed so loudly that Kate blushed and said 'Your English is very good.'

'Oh no, it is not so good. My mother taught me very bad, but please if you could speak slowly.'

'Of course, we must try and remember, but it is difficult to believe that you can't understand us, when you speak so well yourself.' said Kate, very slowly, pronouncing every word carefully.

'You.. must.. speak.. slowly,' Kate said to the children. She didn't realise that she was still speaking very slowly as though to Gustavo, and Alex and Sandra laughed hysterically and Kate had to join in when she realised her own stupidity.

'I am so happy that you are happy family.' Said Gustavo who's remark only increased the hilarity, but he also joined in good humouredly.

Alex showed Gustavo to his room in the attic and Kate asked Sandra to take some towels up at the same time, as she had forgotten them this morning.

The phone rang and Kate answered, but she couldn't understand the person on the other end of the phone, who kept repeating 'Gustavo, por favor.' She went to the bottom of the stairs and shouted, 'Gustavo, telephone.'

It was impossible to do anything. The phone was constantly ringing; either families asking for the tutor, or students repeating down the phone 'profesore por favor.' Never had anyone been so popular.

'What do they all want Gustavo?' Kate asked trying to prepare their evening meal.

'They are like small child. They do not know where bus-a-stop is. They do not know what food is. They are freeze. They do not understand money. They do not understand nothing.'

'Double negative.' Said Kate. 'Either say 'they understand nothing' or 'they don't understand anything' you can't say 'not' and 'nothing' in the same

72

sentence.' Kate stopped abruptly. 'I'm sorry, you have enough problems without me giving you an English lesson. Take no notice of me. If I say we will eat in thirty minutes. Is that convenient?'

'What is convenient,' asked Gustavo.

'Is it not a good time, or will you be doing something else in half an hour or will you not be prepared, ready in half an hour?' Kate said slowly.

'I understand. I understand. Yes, Yes. I will be ready. I am angry.' Said Gustavo enthusiastically.

Kate stopped what she was doing and analysed the word angry and came up with hungry, 'Do you mean you're hungry Gustavo?' Kate responded

'Yes, Yes. I said I am angry.'

'Hungry. Say after me. Ha Ha Hungry.'

'Ha Ha hangry.' Gustavo repeated

'Nearly there.' Said Kate patiently.

The phone rang again and Gustavo rushed towards it. It was just like a farce thought Kate. She called Sandra and Alex downstairs and asked them to lay the table for dinner.

Gustavo came into the kitchen and said, 'Is it possible Sandra and Alex to meet student? To take them bus-a-stop. To school. Tonight?'

They both turned around and said, 'Yes, why not?'

'Good, Good. Thank you. Thank you. Can they come to this house before?'

'Yes of course they can come to the house before.' Said Kate getting the hang of the stilted use of English. 'It's six o'clock. now, so tell them to come at seven thirty, we should have finished dinner by then.'

When Gustavo returned to the table, Alex asked, 'Will you come with us too Gustavo?'

'No, No. I will stay because they must speak English and I will see them tomorrow in Church Also I am very tie-red.'

'Tired.' Said Kate, 'You are tired.' Not tie-red Gustavo.' Kate corrected him.

The phone rang again and Kate sighed as Gustavo left the table to answer it yet again. 'I'm 'tie-red of that damn phone ringing.' Kate said impatiently. 'Let's clear the table and I'll make some coffee. There's some cake or fruit if you're still hungry.'

They could hear Gustavo on the phone and kept hearing their address being spelled out in syllables 'Beech-es Avenoo' he repeated, then in exasperation said. Avenido Bitches.' He turned to Kate and said, 'They will come now. Is that good?'

'Yes, of course. Where will you take them Alex, you must be careful and not too late and help them with their English,' Kate said.

'Don't worry mum, we'll go and get ready so that we can take them out of the way as soon as they arrive.' Alex said, seeing the exasperation on his mother's face.

Kate put the cake on the table, and some fruit, then poured the coffee, just as the doorbell rang.

'I will bring them. You sit. I will bring. Please sit,' he said gesturing with his hands, palms down, pressing towards the floor, trying to be calm, sensing her frustration.

Kate sat and waited with a cup of coffee firmly gripped in her hand. What had she let herself in for? The noise was deafening, and when the kitchen door opened six young Spaniards walked in making the noise of two dozen people at least. They were gesticulating, talking over each other. It looked and sounded chaotic. Gustavo didn't seem to mind the noise. He asked Kate if the students could have water.

'Water. Do they want coffee, hot chocolate, a soft drink? Some cake perhaps. I have biscuits, there's fruit here too. Tell them to sit down.' Kate said this without thinking. Anything to get them to sit and quieten would be good. Kate indicated to them to sit down. She found them folding chairs and stools and handed them plates and cups and glasses before she fetched a jug of water.

Kate began to wash the dishes whilst they were all talking. Alex and Sandra soon came down in response to the noise.

Alex was able to understand some of the conversation. Sandra had more confidence and spoke a little Spanish. 'We'll take them into town, show them where the bus stops are in this area and where to get off. When we get to town, we'll go for a coffee or a soft drink somewhere before we bring them back.' said Alex

They all left leaving more washing up and empty plates. Cake gone, fruit gone, biscuits gone, but it was quiet.

Gustavo and Kate sat in silence drinking coffee. Kate rose to take the cups to the sink. Gustavo followed her.

'Please, Can I help?' said Gustavo..

'Oh no. I'll do them there are only a few,' Kate fussed. Then she thought that it was a bit unkind if he wanted to help. 'Well if you wash them, I'll dry'. He understood the washing bit, so he began to run the water. When they had finished, Kate went upstairs to the bathroom, she only took two steps up when right behind her was Gustavo. 'I'm, - well, I – er…Would you like to sit in the lounge and I'll bring you some beer or would you rather have whiskey?

'Yes. That is good.'

Kate took him into the lounge, sat him down, and searched for the whiskey left over from last Christmas and poured him a drink. She hesitated before she attempted the stairs again, but he didn't follow this time. When she returned he was looking through his file with all the students listed, and she asked if she could help him.

'No. Thank you, my students are all put with their family now. I think they will be happy. I will know tomorrow.'

'Yes.' said Kate with assurance. 'Where do you live in Spain Gustavo?'

'I live in Madrid with my family.'

'With your wife and children?'

'No. With my mother. I have not marry. My mother is angry because I have few children.'

'You have no children' said Kate, understanding that he had no family, but trying to correct his English.

'Yes I have no children. You have children and have no husband?'

'No. He's gone'

'I'm very sorry, you are sad. Yes?'

'No, he's not gone – dead, he's gone away.' Kate explained

'He left without children and you?'

'It wasn't quite like that. I am divorced, and he is married again. The children see him on Sunday'. She said, not realising she was lapsing into his Spanish-English mode of speech.

'Oh. At church, you see him. He lives here?'

'No the children go to his house on Sunday and spend the day with him.'

'Oh, I understand.' Gustavo said.

Conversation was tedious, but they continued to talk and drank until the early hours, long after the children had come in and gone to bed.

Kate was the last to go to bed and she thought what a lovely evening. She had enjoyed Gustavo's company and had felt very comfortable sitting and chatting, even though conversation was slow. It had been interesting.

The month during which the students were here soon passed and the summer holiday was spent going for picnics, visiting all the places of interest close by. Kate was very relaxed and couldn't remember when she had laughed so much. Gustavo hired a car for four months as he needed to get to the local colleges for extra lessons in English for him and to teach Spanish classes in the evenings.

Initially he was an excellent paying guest, but he quickly became a member of their family He often cooked for them, helped the children with their Spanish and they helped him with his English. He was always gently spoken, charming and polite to Kate. His English had improved considerably and they talked about everything; Religion, Politics, relationships, their different backgrounds and cultural differences. Surprisingly they had much in common. Kate enjoyed having Gustavo around for the first two months. He made her feel normal, as though they were a family Having him around also made her think of what they had all been missing since she and Vince, her ex-husband, had split up. Their lives had taken on a new dimension and it was easy to go along with it.

Now it was late October, the last weekend before autumn and winter set in. Gustavo had arranged for them to go on a long hike into the countryside on the Saturday. To walk around the reservoir and over the Tor. They walked for miles, stopping to have tea and sandwiches. He had taken her hand to pull her up hills when she got tired while the two children raced ahead. Suddenly the heavens opened. They were all soaked, to the skin, the rain easily penetrating their shower-proof coats. When they returned to the car.

Gustavo said, 'Take off your clothes, take off your clothes, I have towels.' They all wriggled out of their shower-proof coats and took the first layer of clothing off, leaving them in t-shirts and soggy trousers. Gustavo ushered them into the car and gave them all a towel. He took his coat and sweater off too and got into the car. Kate was shivering in the front passenger seat and Gustavo wrapped the towel around her shoulders, put his left arm around her and rubbed her hair with his towel using his right hand and told Alex and Sandra to towel themselves as dry as they could 'Please do not get cold, we will be not well.'

Kate hadn't felt so cherished in a long time. For a moment she could have cried and had to struggle to keep her emotions in check. This was something she was not prepared for. A friend with his arms around her. She dismissed the incident once they arrived home, keeping busy making them hot drinks and preparing food for their evening meal

After dinner Kate said that she was going for a long bath and then off to bed, as she was tired after the long walk, which was true. As she relaxed in the bath, she started thinking about the day, how much she had enjoyed it, how much fun they had all had. The situation was new to her and she realised that she was beginning to enjoy Gustavo's company. She had liked the way he had touched her earlier in the day when they were in the car drying off.

She was looking at Gustavo in a different light. She had been aroused by being so close to him, a feeling she hadn't experience for a long time. She dismissed the thought, stepped out of the bath and dried herself vigorously trying not to think of Gustavo. It was pointless, he would be gone soon and that would be that. She smiled and thought, perhaps I should take advantage while I can. She reprimanded herself thinking, it would be disastrous for the children and put an end to the good times we've been having. If nothing Else he had given her something to occupy her mind and her aching body.

Kate woke in the middle of the night, sweating and with a raging thirst. A temperature. Flu probably she thought. This wasn't a good scenario. Kate struggled out of bed and went downstairs to find some medication. She took two tablets with some cold water and started to shiver, she felt weak and was overcome with self pity for a moment. She grabbed the box of tissues, wrapped herself up and walked back upstairs. She didn't know if it was self pity or the cold that was making her eyes water and she didn't care. She slumped back on the bed, pulled the duvet over her head and tried to go back to sleep.

The next morning was Sunday. Alex and Sandra had gone to see their dad and Kate was woken by a tapping on the door. She peered at the clock by the side of the bed. Oh no! It was ten o'clock. 'Come in. Who is it?' she said. As she tried to lift her head off the pillow.

Gustavo put his head around the door and said. 'I want to know if you are well. It is very late, you are not in bed at this time on Sunday.'

'I think I have caught a chill after getting soaked yesterday Gustavo. I'll just stay in bed, if you could bring me a hot drink, that would be good and some more tablets in the drawer in the kitchen.'

'You must not worry. I will do everything. I will run you bath and prepare medicine and breakfast. You stay there in the bed until I call to you.'

'No.' Kate started to protest, but she began to cough and reached for the tissues again.

Gustavo was so attentive to Kate's every need. He made her a hot drink, with aniseed in it because, 'It is good for your stomach and will keep you warm,' he said. Kate was too weak to argue, but asked for a cup of coffee too.

'You have nothing to do. I will take care of you.' said Gustavo.

He did take care of Kate too. He gave her some tablets and told her to rest for half an hour then he would make some food. She dozed off and he woke her again half an hour later with a cup of coffee. She was thirsty and drank it almost immediately. He ran a bath for her, helped her to the bathroom and left her to have a bath. She felt just as hot and weak afterwards, but cleaner. Gustavo firmly gripped her hand and helped her back to bed which he had made neat and tidy. He had also made more coffee and toast.

'You're a good nurse Gustavo. I'm so sorry, but I

feel exhausted, you know tired, or should I say tie-red. Do you remember when you first came?'

They both laughed. Gustavo touched her hair, and said. 'I am sorry, it was falling into your coffee, forgive me.' There was an embarrassing silence. Gustavo spoke quietly. 'You must rest.' and he left the room

Kate slept on and off for most of the afternoon. When she woke, she put some old comfortable trousers and a warm sweater on and went downstairs. Gustavo was standing in the kitchen looking pensively out of the window.

'Have you eaten Gustavo?'

Gustavo jumped and turned to face her. 'I did not hear you come downstairs. Do you feel good? I have made rice with chicken. It is good, you must eat. Come, I will serve you. I will eat too. Come. Are you warm? ' He took her arm and felt her hand, rubbed it and said. 'You feel cold. I will fetch blanket.' He made her comfortable in the old kitchen chair and went upstairs.

Kate still felt groggy, but she couldn't sleep any more. She was just feeling down, generally low she thought. It was probably because the nights were longer, or did she have that SAD syndrome? She had to admit, Gustavo being so close around her made her feel weaker than the chill had made her feel. She wished that he wouldn't come so close. Was she falling in lust now? The thought flashed through her mind. She must stop thinking like this. How to ruin a good relationship, she could write the book.

They sat and had dinner together. Kate wrapped in a blanket and Gustavo making fun of her being huddled in the chair. They were both subdued and Kate said. 'Are you well Gustavo, you seem very quiet? Do you think you have caught a chill too?'

'No. No, I am not ill. I have to tell you that I am going back to Madrid at Christmas.' He blurted out this information and looked at his empty plate.

She could feel the tears welling in her eyes. She turned away and took a tissue from the box and blew her nose to conceal her disappointment and surprise at this piece of news. Kate eventually spoke. 'Of course, you must go back to be with your family at Christmas Gustavo. We'll miss you. Will you stay in Madrid for good, or will you return?' Kate tried to sound nonchalant

'I don't think so, but I would like to ask one favour for you. I would like you and Alex and Sandra to come with me to my house with my mother and my grandmother and my sister and my aunt and my nieces and nephews and my brother-in-law. I think that is all, but perhaps my uncle will visit. I do not know yet.' Gustavo said hurriedly.

'I think there are enough people at your house for Christmas Gustavo. It will be difficult for us all to go too. You are very kind to invite us, but I'm sure your mother will be happy to have you home for a while.'

'She has asked for you to go. She wants to know the family I have been living with. I have told her all about you and Alex and Sandra.' Gustavo looked at her directly and said quietly 'Please, I would like you to go too. I would like you to ask the children.'

'I don't think that's a good idea Gustavo. Let's not talk about it now, not while I'm feeling so ill.'

'Oh! I am sorry. I am sorry. You must go back to your bed and I will bring you a drink and medicine. Please forget what I have said.' He cupped her elbow and helped her to the stairs. She felt this overwhelming tenderness towards him and stood there for a moment. She thought he was going to follow her, but he turned and hesitated, 'Are you going up the stairs alone, will you be okay?' He looked troubled and took a step back.'

Yes. I'll be fine Gustavo. Thank you for dinner and taking care of me today. It was very kind of you'

'I have enjoyed. I wish you would change your mind, but I will not talk about Madrid.'

That had been a lie. Once she was feeling better, he talked constantly about going back to Madrid, about the shops, about Real Madrid, how he would go to the stadium to watch the famous football team play, about the processions, until Alex and Sandra turned on her too and started pleading with her, doing everything in their power to make her agree to going to Madrid for Christmas. That's all she heard, Madrid,! Christmas! please!

The last few weeks had been different. Since she had been ill after their little expedition. Gustavo had begun to stand too close to her. She loved it, but found it difficult to seize the moment. She would never have done that when she was a very young woman and couldn't do it now although from what she heard on the radio and Television and read in magazines, women did take the initiative these days, but she didn't have the confidence. She thought that it would spoil the relationship, both with her and with Alex and Sandra and she didn't want that. He had even taken her out for dinner She had fussed over her appearance for the first time in years. He had said she looked pretty, but had been very quiet all night and she had to force the conversation.

She was frustrated by the situation and disappointed. She really shouldn't get herself into such a state. She wanted him sexually. It was obvious to her, why wasn't it obvious to him. Why didn't he kiss her, she could take it from there. What was she talking about? Where was all this confidence coming from? She hadn't had a man for some years now. She laughed out loud at the thought. He hadn't even tried to persuade her to go to Madrid. Why should she want to go and meet his mother and family? She didn't know them, although she thought they must be lovely people. Christmas was a family time, not to have another family, a new family, a strange family with you for a whole two weeks.

A week later when they were in the kitchen preparing breakfast, he had taken her hand and looked at her. All he said was, 'Please come.' They weren't even talking about Madrid at the time. He quickly let go of her hand and walked away. His behaviour was uncharacteristic. She was beginning to think she was losing his friendship and that was a painful thought.

The pressure from them all was too much to bear. She began to feel worn down with the continual chatter about Madrid. 'Just all of you shut up and go away.' She said one particularly miserable Saturday. She was so surprised when they all said okay. Put on their coats and went out.

Peace and quiet reigned for most of the day. She cleaned the house, prepared the dinner and sat down with her book. They were gone for about four hours and she was getting worried. Had she gone too far, shouted too loudly, been too angry? She went into the kitchen to make a drink when the back door opened and they all came skulking in. Gustavo had a bottle in his hand, Alex was holding a bunch of flowers and Sandra had a box with posh cakes in it she assumed looking at the small white cardboard box tied up with thin ribbon. They were all grinning, but looked anxious and stood waiting for someone to speak.

Gustavo who had been looking at the ground, looked up and met Kate's stare, 'We have been very naughty. Mea Culpa. It is my fault.' Said Gustavo sheepishly

'For goodness sake, what happened?' she said thinking there had been an accident, or something had gone wrong.

'Mum, Mum,' Alex piped up taking charge of the situation. 'Gustavo has booked tickets for all of us to go to Madrid for Christmas and we encouraged him. We want to go and we want you to go too. Please, please be reasonable.' He pleaded.

She was so relieved it wasn't anything more serious that she smiled and put her arms out to give them all a hug Alex and Sandra came together and gave her such an excited squeeze. 'We're off to get packing Ma!' Alex shouted as they put down their gifts and ran upstairs. Gustavo said, 'You are not angry Kate?' He stepped forward and she put her arms round his shoulders and gave him a hug too. He held on just a little too long for Kate. She wanted to lean on him turn her face towards him encourage him to kiss her or something. Anything, she was desperate now.

He quickly kissed her cheek, moved back and said 'Thank you. You will enjoy I promise. You have made me and my family very happy. I will ring my mother and tell her.'

Kate busied herself and thought of the last moment with Gustavo. She had to admit experiencing that deep rooted ache when you feel sexually attracted to someone, all those fluttering feelings believing that you would melt into each other. How ridiculous she thought. He wants to take us to see his family that's all. I'm reading far too much into it. She couldn't help feeling a little disappointed with his brief kiss.

Everyone was so excited but Kate. She was beginning to dread Christmas coming. Gustavo was fussing round, telling her what to pack, saying, 'that will be warm,' 'you look very pretty in that.' They had so little time. Gustavo had booked the tickets on the 16th December and they flew out on 23rd. The week flew by and Kate's apprehension increased. She kept her thoughts to herself because Alex and Sandra were so excited.

They arrived in Madrid on 23rd December and took a taxi to one of the main streets in the city centre. Gustavo paid the taxi driver who put their cases by a huge wooden door with wrought iron fittings. Gustavo pressed one of the buttons and spoke into the intercom and the lock was released on the door. They walked in and through the dimness of the corridor, she saw the concierge came forward walk past them and put their cases in a lift and closed the door.

'Where are our cases going?' Alex asked not wanting to lose his belongings.

'Don't worry, they will be taken to the apartment.' Gustavo said as he ushered them into another lift and pressed the button for the third floor. Kate felt very nervous, but Gustavo was wearing one continuous smile and once out of the lift, encouraged her to turn left down another corridor. Reassured, she walked on. Suddenly he was in control and this was unfamiliar ground for her. They walked down the corridor past many doors until they came to 217. Gustavo rang the bell and a young girl answered wearing a blue dress and apron. She was excited to see Gustavo and greeted him with a kiss on each cheek. She indicated for Kate and the children to come in and beckoned them to follow her giving them a warm smile They were led through a long dark sitting room into the dining room, through a corridor and into another sitting room where a greying lady in a black dress sat in a dark wooden chair.

This must be his mother thought Kate. Very Spanish, and noted how dignified the household seemed. Kate and the children waited until Gustavo greeted his mother. He turned to Kate and her children and said with an air of achievement, 'This is my Mother Maria. Mama this is Kate and her children Alex the young man and Sandra the young lady.'

Maria, Gustavo's mother grasped them all in turn and kissed them on both cheeks and said. 'Please, you must forgive me. My English it is bad now. I do not use it, but you are welcome. My son writes many things about you and your kindness. Please Kate, can I say Kate? Please sit here. You must call me Maria.' Maria sent the young girl in the blue dress out, with instructions in Spanish and then they all sat down, but Maria again spoke to her son in Spanish and he took the children out. Kate didn't feel uneasy, but the house was impressive and so was Maria. It was obvious that the children had been taken out so that they could talk privately and Kate was right,

Maria was very friendly and hospitable, but asked all sorts of questions and Kate found herself talking quite freely and openly about herself. The maid brought in olives and a glass of wine and some bread with a spicy tomato sauce. Kate wasn't hungry, but she sipped the wine and popped an olive in her mouth to be polite. Then all of a sudden, Maria said ' Our talk, it has been of interest Kate, but you will need to be in your room to be ready for dinner. This is at eight o'clock I will see you here.' Before Kate knew it she was dismissed and shown to her room to change for dinner.

There was a tap on the door and Sandra came in. 'Oh Mum, you should see the fountain and tomorrow we're going to the Prado, the Art gallery. You know the famous one. The cakes are lovely and we went into this bar and had fish. Mum you must go out tonight and see it all and have you seen the size of this flat. There are four bathrooms. They're having guests for dinner, aunts and uncles apparently.'

'One thing at a time Sandra. How many did you say are coming for dinner?'

'About nine I think Gustavo said.' Sandra replied.

'But that makes fourteen altogether.'

'The dining room will hold that easily.' Replied Sandra confidently

Kate took a little more time preparing herself, and told Sandra and Alex to do the same. When Kate was ready she walked back to the sitting room where she had been talking to Maria. Gustavo and his mother were having what looked like a heated discussion in

Spanish, but they stopped abruptly as she entered. Maria rose and took Kate's arm. 'We have some guests tonight, I think you will like these people they are uncles and aunts of Gustavo.' Kate assured her that she would be pleased to meet them.

The evening was a very noisy one, everyone talking at the same time, usually asking Kate about herself. Sometimes the questions they asked were quite personal; about her marriage and her job as a teacher, but the evening was a huge success, despite the language problems. Gustavo had hovered round her all night; helping out with any difficulties she had understanding his many relatives. His intention had been to make her more comfortable, but in fact he had made her more nervous. He always stood so close to her that she could feel the heat from his body. He kept touching her arm, filling up her wine glass, doing small kindnesses. Despite this, she had enjoyed the evening. She was glad when people started saying their goodbyes, but making Kate promise to visit them for dinner before her holiday was over Maria took the children into another room to show them some photographs and left Gustavo and Kate alone.

'You have a lovely family, Gustavo.' Kate said smiling broadly

'It is true, you like them? My uncle he working with pigs, my sister, she teach, like you,' Gustavo droned on about his family.

'It is true. I like them' mocked Kate when she interrupted his list of his family. She was annoyed with him for being so close all evening, making her feel claustrophobic She didn't listen to the explanation of his family tree, but stared at him intensely wondering what he was thinking, wondering why she felt so attracted to him at this particular moment. How she wouldn't mind if he stood close to her right now She let the strap of her dress fall onto her arm. He never flinched. Kate stood up, said 'Goodnight' and walked out.

Gustavo frowned and looked disappointed. .

Kate almost tore her clothes off and threw them on a chair in the corner, put on her night clothes and went to find a bathroom. She met Sandra on the corridor who was still bubbling over with enthusiasm. 'Oh Mum, you should see the villa they've got in the south of Spain, it's gorgeous. Tia....

'Who?' interrupted Kate.

'She asked us to call her Tia, it means Aunt in Spanish, she wants us to go there for a holiday, she says that it's too big for just her and Gustavo. Oh Mum, could we go, she's really sweet. Me and Alex could come on our own next year with Gustavo if you don't want to come. You wouldn't mind would you?'

Kate said nothing; glared at Sandra; went into the bathroom and slammed the door. Alex came down the corridor to find Sandra. 'What was that?' asked Alex.

'Don't ask me, she's as mad as hell, have you said anything to her?' asked Sandra.

'I haven't seen her since we arrived,' Alex replied.' You don't think Gustavo made a pass at her do you? He's had quite a bit to drink'

'Don't be silly Alex, he wouldn't do that, not after all this time anyway Mum and Gustavo aren't like that. They're such good friends. 'He's not at all sexy.'

'You're right.' said Alex.

The next ten days were hectic they visited everyone and everything that was of interest to them. Although they were exhausted, another party had been arranged for January 5th which is the celebration of the Three Kings, called 'Reyez'. Like 'Christmas Day' in England. They exchanged gifts on this day, and Kate had been out to buy small gifts for everyone and for once had given Gustavo the slip. She had enjoyed the experience, but she wanted it to be over, to get back to normal. She wasn't sure how she would cope with her return to England. She half wished that Gustavo was staying in Madrid. Now she was feeling emotional and irritable, but everyone had been so kind and she thought she was going to cry.

Gustavo had begged to go with her to the shops, but she had been adamant about going alone. She just wanted her own space; to be on her own for a short while. She felt so weak and helpless when he was there The situation had reached a point where she couldn't think straight when he was in the same room as her. She hadn't eaten all day, her feet ached and she felt tense and upset. She wrapped up all the gifts and dressed quickly so that she wouldn't be late for dinner. Lots of noise could be heard coming from the dining room as she approached and through glass doors she could see lots of people. She jumped as the glass doors opened unexpectedly. It was Gustavo.

'Ah, kiss me Kate.' He called enthusiastically trying to get her in the mood for the party and the night of celebration ahead

'Don't be stupid.' She said quietly to him so that no one else could hear and pushed past him in a white fury. How dare he, she thought. She couldn't hide the anger on her face and everyone came towards her to asking if she was alright. This was the last straw, she turned round to face Gustavo, and whispered, 'idiot,' pushed past him again and went back to her room apologising, saying she wouldn't be a moment. That she had forgotten something. She had, she had forgotten the gifts and her manners it seemed.

Gustavo shrugged his shoulders and said 'It is nothing. One moment I will fetch her, she will be back. Please drink' he said the same in Spanish and then walked towards Kate's room.

Kate was pushing her things into a case, tears of rage trickled down her cheeks and she wasn't making much sense.

'How stupid, how bloody stupid. No man has ever got me into this state. It serves me right, I've only got myself to blame, why should I think that he should want me. I've almost thrown myself at him, well at least twice I've been so close, he could have kissed me at least, but no he's such a bloody gentleman. Damn him. Kate said all this to herself before Gustavo burst in.

'What is the matter? Why you angry? Please, Please.' he moved closer to her and put his arm around her.

'I'm just tie-red and confused she said. You have been so attentive and I think it's time for you to stay in Spain and for us to get on with our lives. I have grown very fond of you Gustavo and the situation is very difficult, you are so kind and I think I've read too much into our relationship. I'm so sorry and I feel so foolish.' He tightened his grip on her, put his other arm round her and laughed.

'You will marry me please, you will marry me?'

'I'll what! After all I've ...You. Never. I...when did you decide this'

I decide 3 or 4 month ago, but Mama, she was happy because I want to marry, but she must see you.'

'Your mother! What about me?'

You came for me so well and we laugh so much together. I knew you love me.' Not another word was spoken. He kissed her once twice, again and again, each kiss lasting longer than the last. They separated for a few brief moments while they undressed.

When they rejoined the party, everyone was chatting, but getting impatient having to wait for their dinner. They were all given a cold glass of champagne. Kate looked at Gustavo. He said, 'I have to say toast, I have to say toast.' Kate was no longer angry, she looked happy and she touched Gustavo's arm affectionately.

'Where have you been?' asked Alex and Sandra simultaneously.

'None of your business,' said Kate

'What have you been up to Mum?' said Alex

'I believe that you will be having your holiday in the Villa permanently,' replied Kate

'Are you saying what I think you're saying?' said Sandra, looking first at Gustavo then her mother. 'But he's not sexy, neither does he look like your knight in shining armour Are you going to be good friends?' said Sandra making the inverted comma marks in the air when she said friends.

'So we are, very good friends, as any married couple are.'

THE RIVER
Georgia Varjas

I didn't want to go back. I had left seventeen years ago, and swore with anger and passion that I would never go back. Then, the letter arrived. Unmarked, unscented and I didn't recognise the handwriting but then why should I? I hadn't seen any of them for many years.

I tore open the envelope and felt the thin paper. A short message, several words crossed out, basic English misspelt. Did they think I had forgotten my mother tongue? My eyes scrolled down to the signature, one word. Melita. I repeated the name to place the wife, daughter or cousin. I walked around my kitchen mumbling her name. Then, it came back to me. Melita was my uncle's second wife. I hadn't forgotten; I had simply buried all of them deep into the ground. I sat down to read the note. Death in a letter must be hard to state but Melita did it in five lines.

The brothers had been close, my father, Viktor just a year older. Viktor and Robert had married two women from the same village on the same day.

They both had a moustache, and both were fishermen. It was almost like a plot from a B movie.

In the letter, Melita said that my uncle had died in his sleep and had left me a small valise. I imagined a damaged leather suitcase with two rusty silver clasps that didn't close properly. I was sure it would be stuffed with sepia photos, some keys, maybe a watch, letters tied with string and a pair of binoculars. Why should I travel back? For useless relics from a man I hated? But it was the last sentence of the note that was the most intriguing. Melita insisted I return, not for the funeral, or the memorial service but to hear her words. I shook my head. I had heard plenty of words; everybody had their truth to tell and I didn't want to hear another version of it.

What can I say? Over the years, I had created an immense barrier against returning, yet I went. I was entwined with curiosity, almost morbid, like the 'car crash syndrome' when you can't resist slowing down to stare at an accident on the road. Curiosity is such a basic emotion, full of moral and judgemental connotations. Was it the truth I was seeking, or some disturbed fascination about the secrets of my family?

The flight was delayed and I arrived after midnight. I stepped out of the airport into that freezing November night, cold enough to threaten snow. The taxi drove through the deserted streets and I stared at the lights on the bridges, pretty twinkling lights, disguising the heavy black silence that lay over the city. The driver kept gazing at me in his rear-view mirror; I guess he was inquisitive about a woman on her own and my staccato language use. I didn't want to talk; I felt a weight descend upon me. I began to doubt my reasons for being here. I cursed myself for coming, for indulging in such false, empty curiosity.

I slept well - I was surprised. I took a shower and wrapped in a towel, opened the curtains of the hotel window. Outside was the river. Already there were small patches of ice forming, like weak tablets, broken and pushed aside by the long cargo barges. It made me shiver. I got dressed and went out onto the street to find a café. The sweet smells of freshly baked cakes always excited my appetite. I was hungry and devoured four of my favourite pastries, washing them down with two large milky coffees.

Alert and pleasantly fortified by the sugar and caffeine, I rang Melita. I had practised a hundred times my words to her, but when she answered, I couldn't remember any of them.

'I'm here in the city, I'll rent a car and come up to you.'

'There is a train.' Melita said.

'No, I'll drive.'

'I haven't opened the case.' She said.

I didn't know what to say. Was she just trying to add some melodramatic mystery?

'I'll see you after lunch,' I said and hung up.

I rented a Volkswagen Polo and headed out across the river to the east. From there, I turned north to make the forty-minute drive to the village where I grew up. The landscape was wintry; bare dark–limbed trees, empty fields with white frosty patches creeping upon the black earth, and crows, cawing their plaintive cries. I drove through several villages without looking at my old childhood playgrounds.

I stopped the car one hundred metres away from the large family house. Three generations had lived there. The brothers, my father and uncle had divided the house to accommodate their wives and children. Divided with curtains, blankets, and large strips of plywood. No secrets in our house. Every sound was heard and interpreted.

Since my parents had died, since my cousins had disappeared to Australia - since then - it was only the garden that appeared different. Concrete had been poured everywhere. Four neglected flowerpots stood beside the front door. My father had loved flowers; dahlias and roses were his passion. My mother cultivated marrows, asparagus and tomatoes. Now - not a speck of colour remained.

It wasn't just poverty, it was a greyness of mind, an exhaustion in fighting with the endless hypocritical regimes. Lies and promises, and the disillusionment of love and life covered the house on all sides.

I started up the engine of the car, ready to turn it around and go back to the city and fly home. I saw Melita come up the path, a blanket wrapped around her head and shoulders. I rolled the car forward and parked outside the entrance.

'Shall I take your bag?' She asked holding out a hand.

'No. No luggage.'

'Erika, you're not staying? I made up a bed for you.'

I didn't answer but I thought, no, never again.

I followed her into the kitchen. There was some bright new Formica furniture, matching white and yellow cupboards, tables and chairs. I took off my coat, folding it over my lap and sat down at the table. I didn't wait for the invite and I didn't intend to stay long. Melita stood by the sink filling the kettle; she was still an attractive woman in her early sixties, tall and slim. She was dressed in jeans and a jumper, not designer, neither the market. She wore a little makeup around her pale blue eyes, a touch of pink lipstick, her nails neatly manicured and lacquered, she looked good. Was this a woman in mourning?

I looked around the kitchen; the old hearth had been bricked up and painted over, blinds instead of net curtains draped the windows. Then, I saw the suitcase.

'What do you want to talk to me about?' I asked, not taking my eyes off the case.

'There's nothing in it,' Melita said, her eyes also fixed upon the valise.

'How do you know it's empty?'

'It's not heavy.'

'Why did you drag me here?' I felt anger rising.

'Because it was his last wish.'Melita poured out steaming coffee into two cups. I got up and moved to the door.

'You tricked me Melita, and you forced me to come here for that empty case?'

'You were curious Erika.' She was so calm I felt rage.' Perhaps, you thought he left you some money…don't worry, it's normal to think that.'

A sly smile crossed her face. 'Please sit down Erika, and listen.'

I rubbed my forehead, exasperated; I knew I shouldn't have come. On what stupid whim did I book the flight? Was it greed? Did I expect to receive a fortune from the man I hated most in this world?

We drank the coffee in silence. Then Melita spoke.

'Do you want to see the house?'

'Why did you cement up the garden? It looks…it's so dissolute.'

'Robert and I don't…didn't enjoy gardening.'

I was getting restless, all this superficial talk. What was there left to say now that both men were dead?

'Erika, you need to know…'she paused, squeezed her lips together, gestured her hands in the air.' For your peace of mind, for a better life.'

'I heard your version before Melita, what's new?'

'Viktor and Robert were being pressurised by local gangsters to give up their fishing territory.'

'Gangsters? Aren't you being a bit dramatic?'

'There were rivals - competitors who wanted to steal the lucrative fishing area that your father and Robert owned. The officials and the river police had been bribed to persecute the brothers.'

Melita shook her head at me like I was a child who couldn't understand the serious adult information she was giving me.

I got up; I had to get some fresh air. It was too much of a conspiracy, too complex a story, seventeen years after the event. I put on my coat, stepped to the door and turned to look at Melita. My keys were on the table, I said nothing and closed the door behind me. The cold air hit my face like a sheet of water; I pulled up the collar of my coat and walked down the path and out of the front garden. Nothing had changed in the street and instinctively I headed for the river. The sun was setting behind a thick layer of barren trees and pink clouds. A lone seagull screeched across the sky. I stood at the bank of the river; a thousand memories poured into my mind. Summer picnics, paddling and searching for frogs, jumping up to catch dragonflies, and picking fresh berries from the bushes. Happy moments in childhood, all gone, all vanished into a library in my head that I redecorated every few years.

It's true, in those last years of my fathers' life, the brothers were always arguing, but it was friendly…I thought. Friendly pushing and shoving, with a beer in your hand and a laugh in your throat, like men do, like brothers do. The night they went out, the night my father died, drowned in the freezing river; they had argued, shouted at each other, but they went to fish.

I remember in the afternoon as they repaired the nets, they bickered and laughed. It was their style. But that night, Robert said that my father had been drunk, again. Drunk and singing. He had stood up in the nine metre boat and started doing a Csardas - a knees up.

I wiped back the tears with my sleeve before they froze into tiny icicles on my cheek. Melita was beside me, a handkerchief in her hand.

'It was an accident Erika, no one was to blame. The cruel truth is…'

She stopped to gaze out onto the dark river.' They both died happy.' Melita touched my arm and I took the paper tissue from her.' After your father died, those thieves took away the fishing license from Robert. They had been harassing them, taking photos, doing spot checks.'

'How long had this been going on?' I asked.

'More than a year. We believe that one of them, probably one of those bandits, got to your father; threatened him, pushed him over the edge. He began to drink heavily and find excuses not to go fishing.'

'Your husband was a drinker too!' I felt pathetic as soon as I said it. I remembered telling my father to quit; he was too old to be fishing nights, sticking his arms and legs into that troublesome river.

Neither of us said a word, but my childish outburst hung in the icy air before my eyes. Melita sighed.

'I call them Mafioso's, these men that hounded Robert and Viktor. Every time they took the boat out, there was always someone waiting, trying to find an illegal technicality to ban them from fishing on the river.'

'Why did I blame Robert, why did I believe he pushed him in?'

'Erika, everybody blamed Robert.' She dropped her arm from mine and turned to me.' He was his brother's keeper. His children blamed him and abandoned him, went to Australia. How do you think he felt?' She took out another handkerchief and blew her nose.

'You stayed.'

'Yes, I saw how Robert struggled to maintain the balance between those criminals and the difficulties he had with your father.'

I watched how her breath vanished like smoke into the frosty air. The sun had set; there was a silvery slate-coloured light, like a shadow settled on the dark moving river. That damn river!

My father loved to weave stories about how the weather in the Alps, three or four hundred kilometres away, could change the condition of the river before it even happened. He would listen to the radio; search the newspapers to make notes about snowfalls, heavy rains and storms. Then, in the spring he would explain to me the reason for the flooding.

'You see Erika,' and he would stroke my hair as he spoke.' The river has flooded because between January 10th and the end of the month, there was a terrible and continuous fall of snow in the Alps.'

As a child, I believed him, relished his tales of the river, and admired his knowledge. Later, I knew that every spring the river would swell, often flood. Rushing through the villages and towns stealing bushes, branches, chickens and puppies. Dragging anything and everything in its way. You couldn't swim in the river it was so fast. We used to joke about it. If you got into the water, you wouldn't be able to get out until you reached Africa!

'Come Melita, let's go in now.' I took hold of her arm and together we walked slowly back up to the house. Once inside, we removed our coats, sat at the kitchen table and slowly melted, our hands and faces turning red. Finally, I spoke.

'I am sorry, I shouldn't have made an enemy of you all these years. I know my father was a drunk, I guess I had to blame someone…and…'

'And I was the nearest in line,'Melita said, her gaze hard upon me.

We sat together for another hour, but we had nothing to say to each other. Small talk between estranged people doesn't go far. I headed back to the city and spent the night in my hotel room. I ordered a sandwich from room service and went to bed early. Emotions and the cold bring on tiredness.

The next morning, I checked out of the hotel, my flight wasn't until six o'clock in the evening, so I left my case in the luggage room and headed for the coffee shop. It was a grey overcast freezing day. The people on the street walked fast, huddled inside heavy coats and scarves. In the café, after another sweet and delicious breakfast, I gazed out onto the river. That damn river!

I paid the bill, grabbed my coat, and walked out of the café. I headed for the riverfront, I didn't know why; it was like my demons were calling me.

I increased my pace. I felt excited like a child. The ticket office had just opened and I was the only person buying. The young woman who issued the ticket raised her eyes but not her head.

'Are you sure, it's freezing today, colder than usual, it might even snow.'

I waited another fifteen minutes before a steward came and let me get on the tourist boat. I wasn't going to be put off. I had made up my mind to take this ride through the city and look at life from the river's point of view. To ride on top of that river that took so much away from me. Twenty minutes later, a group of Japanese tourists arrived and at last, the captain decided to depart from the pier.

Since the day my father died, I swore I would never go near the river. I swore I would never come back to the country. Yet this morning, none of those boundaries seemed valid. I had obstructed myself, created a barrier between my history and me, worse still, limited myself. I realised that now the past doesn't exist. It is only the way I think about it that is relevant.

The cruise boat headed north and I sat inside by a large window staring out at the waters. The river had a greenish brown colour, slow and sludgy, reflecting only the heavy grey sky above. I let my mind go blank.

I wasn't going to drift back in time or walk that dangerous plank of nostalgia. Melita said that my father had died singing and laughing. How many of us get to do that?

I pulled out of my bag the envelope that Melita had given me. After all, there was something left for me. I opened it and pulled out two A4 black and white photographs. The top picture featured my father, my uncle and me, aged fourteen. Three of us sat in a row in the fishing vessel. The boat was close to a small pier. It was summer and I wore a swimsuit, the brothers wore shorts. All of us were smiling. Behind us the river flowed.

In the second photograph, it was winter, ice floes sat upon the water like molehills. Snow was falling and the background was white with dark skeletal trees. We were thickly clothed from head to foot. Our eyes were lit up with happiness. My father stood next to his brother, their arms around each other. I stood in front of them, all teeth. The fishing boat was behind us and it looked like it was stuck in the ice.

I stared at the photographs for a long time, not thinking just taking in the detail, not remembering but enjoying the present. Finally, I put the pictures back into the envelope and into my bag. I pulled up the collar of my coat and went up onto the deck to stare out at the river again.

A SWEET SMILE
Rosemary Westwell

Elaine bit her lip determined to stop the tears from falling. She stared in disbelief as the giggling school girls glared at her, their young faces sneering. They gathered together more closely, their shiny heads meeting as they whispered in their huddle. The ringleader, Harper, put her thin hand over her mouth and whispered another evil suggestion. Her classmates nodded and giggled, hugging each other in delight.

Elaine sighed. She had no idea what they would do to her next and she wished she did not care, but she did. It hurt, it really hurt. She had never come across such unbridled hate before. Although always lonely in her isolated life on the farm, that loneliness was comforting. She could explore the fields and copses on her father's land to her heart's content. She could pick posies of wild flowers and watch the kestrels hover above in the clear blue sky. She could run to the top of the hill and let the wind ruffle her hair. She felt alive. The wilder the weather, the more thrilling it was for her. When the rain splashed her chilled cheeks she knew she was alive, a living breathing part of an exciting world that she eagerly looked forward to exploring

But now, now she was imprisoned in this cold dark boarding house. Her parents were keen to give her a good education and it was this school that was supposed to be the best in the county. She had never thought that receiving a good education meant such suffering. She had seen pictures of prisoners of war in some of the books in her Dad's library and now she felt she could understand how those poor prisoners felt. The daily routine was fixed. There was no place for feeling free to do what you wanted. Forced to get up in the mornings while it was still dark, she learned to wait until the other girls finished in the bathroom. She had had enough of water being splashed in her face and the threat of having her head pushed down into the toilet bowl again. No, she would wait, wait until there was only one girl left. She could probably tackle one girl on her own. She would walk to the opposite end of the row of basins and wash – the soap not lathering in the now freezing water. It was hard to dress in the dormitory with so many cold pairs of eyes staring maliciously at her self-consciousness as she tried to keep young body covered at all times while she struggled to put on her school uniform. They were already fully dressed. They only waited so they could be entertained by her struggles. When they had had enough they traipsed off together in a self satisfied pack. Elaine trailed behind to join the group as they lined up for breakfast. As she stood behind Anne, a slim blond-haired soon-to-be actress, Anne suddenly looked behind her. She grimaced when she saw Elaine, pinched her nose and complained bitterly of the smell. Elaine knew she did not smell any more than the rest of them. She had had a bath the previous night and all the clothes she had put on were fresh. In a ripple, her class mates joined in the complaints, staring back at her while she stood her ground, blinking hard.

Day in and day out this was to be her life while she was at this boarding school. How she wished she could be at home, climbing fences, running in the fields feeling the breeze on her cheeks. The only time she had to do what she wanted was one hour after school and in the weekends while the other boarders were taken out by their parents. Elaine's parents had to work every weekend and she understood this. There were no outings for her at the weekend. She could not leave the school premises in this free time, so there was no exploring for her yet. She sat at her desk waiting for prep time. She had little else to do. It was no good trying to go outside and join in with her classmates' play – once she arrived their play turned into games of how to humiliate Elaine. So Elaine sat at her desk and started writing. From the beginning she decided to write about the good times, days on the farm, helping with the lambing, caring for the injured birds she sometimes found in the fields. She wrote about her Mum and Dad and how it felt to be free. She even wrote stories about how prisoners of war felt and how much they treasured freedom afterwards. In her few years of experience she already had some insight into what it must have been like.

Then, in their English class that morning the teacher gave everyone a sheet of paper. It was a writing competition organized by the local newspaper. Elaine sighed. The whole class knew that Harper, the teacher's pet, would have to write the best essay, yet again. Elaine had soon learned to avoid being punished by her peers by writing anything that would be better than Harper's attempt. Elaine had to agree that Harper's compositions were good, quite good but Elaine could not help feeling that although the stories were well crafted, they lacked soul, they lacked imagination. Elaine found it difficult to understand how someone could like English and do so well at it while maintaining a mechanical precise approach that made her stories sound clinical, almost clichés. Elaine rather enjoyed the challenge of making her attempts just slightly less proficient that Harper's. Elaine would write and write savouring every word and creating a story that made her feel like laughing, crying – expressing whatever emotions she evoked. Then she would rewrite the composition in school girl style, making some of her words more mundane, dampening its spirit.

Today, the composition was going to be different. This time the newspaper was holding a competition asking children their age to write a composition about 'Freedom'. Elaine had learned to sit at the back of the class so that there was no one behind her to kick her chair or torment her. Today she watched Harper who always sat at the front, sit bolt upright, grinning and staring around the class at her mates. She was always top of the class in English and she had no doubt that she would win the competition. Her classmates looked at her adoringly. They too, knew that the prize was hers. That night, for prep, they all wrote their stories. The following day they handed in their essays. Elaine passed hers forward to Fran who was sitting in front of her. Fran turned round, grimaced and gingerly held Elaine's paper at the top corner, as if trying to avoid being contaminated by such a disgusting object before passing it to the girl in front of her. Elaine looked down at her desk; the teacher was completely unaware of this activity because she was busy collecting the other papers.

At assembly two weeks later, the headmistress coughed into the microphone. All her staff sat primly in a row behind her. Sitting in the middle was a strange man. She introduced the special visitor as the editor of the local newspaper who was going to award the prize to the winner of the competition. The editor stood up, a tall slim man in a pin-striped suit. He talked about the competition and about the winning essay. He praised the language, the style, the wonderful imagination. Harper sat up listening eagerly. She beamed. The editor praised the way the writer had got into the mind of someone who was imprisoned. Harper frowned. Her friends looked at each other, puzzled. Elaine's cheeks flushed. He finally asked Elaine, the winner, to come up onto the stage to receive the prize.

With trembling legs, Elaine stood up carefully ignoring the glares and daggers of hate that swept from her peers' eyes. Finally up on the stage she received the envelope. The editor asked if she would like to say a few words. Elaine nodded. Now was her chance. She turned to face the school. Her heart throbbed loudly but she was determined. There was no place for timidity now. She thanked the editor, told him how much she enjoyed writing and turned to the school and said how she especially wanted to thank a particular group of girls in the school, and one girl especially. The tirade of words that flowed from her lips surpised even herself. She thanked her peers who had made her life so unbearable with their cruelty. She listed every nasty deed they had done. She finally thanked them for teaching her what it was like to be stripped of freedom. She thanked Harper especially for this new experience and now she, Elaine, had a lot of material to write many more stories and articles. She looked at the editor and suggested that she may, one day, become a journalist. He nodded enthusiastically. The headmistress and the staff, sat immobile, their cheeks flushed, their eyes flashing.

Elaine smiled a sweet smile at her evil peers, walked off the stage and into the corridor. She phoned her parents.

LEONIE'S SEARCH FOR LOVE
Rosemary Westwell

Leonie stared at the face in the mirror. Yes, it was young, the cheeks were pink, the eyes a sort of grey, the nose a bit small and upturned and the mouth small. It was not ideal. She held the long strands of the mousy-brown hair that framed her face and brought them up to the top of her head. Yes, she would look better with her hair up. She spent another hour experimenting with her hairstyle, putting on make-up and taking it off again until she was finally satisfied with 'the look'. This was the best she could do. She pushed open her wardrobe door. She would wear the blue tonight. She could still fit into it, and she always felt relaxed in it. It hugged her hips a little too much, but it showed off her slim legs – her one good quality. She swung round in front of the long mirror. She supposed she was ready to go to the party. She sighed.

She had been to so many parties before and so many of them had been disasters. Either all her friends were immediately clinched with their steady boyfriends and she was left high and dry alone, the only person in the house, alone or there were just too many drunken boys with groping hands pulling at her clothes and grabbing for her most embarrassing parts. She blushed to think of them. She shook her head.

She had been out on more blind dates than she cared to remember. There was that extremely shy boy at the office who did not say a whole word for the entire date. He managed to hold her hand and that was it. He wasn't worth the trouble. There was that loud-mouthed Henry who tried to sweep her off her feet but it was only too obvious he was trying to show off to his mates who cheered and roared as he danced with her and of course, there was that devoted Danny with the big brown eyes who unfortunately laughed so like a grunting pig to her she could not stand the idea of hearing him laugh again. She had had her fill of internet dating too. They were always much more ghastly looking than their photos, had a high squeaky voice she never expected or were only after her money and soon disappeared when they realized she didn't have any.

One day she would find her true love. It was in the cards. The fortune teller at the fair had told her. She would just have to keep looking. At least she had been taught some of the tricks of the trade where dating was concerned. Her kind friends at college had felt sorry for her. Janet, now firmly ensconced with Bill, took her aside at a party one time and gave her some very good advice – advice that she had tried to follow every since.

'Stand away from the crowds, on your own. Keep the conversation flowing by asking you partner all about themselves. How long they had known the hosts, where they worked, what kind of car they drove, what they thought of going to parties. Confide in them just how you feel. Don't put on any airs and graces. Don't try to impress. Just say to them how you would much rather a quiet conversation over a drink in a café than having to shout above loud music at a party. Admit that your weekends are boring because you don't go out much…' There was no end to the advice that Janet had given, and there was no doubt that it had worked for Janet because, after all, Janet with her hairy upper lip and large ears was no great beauty but Bill clearly loved her – tall, handsome Bill had soon fallen for her charms. Leonie had already had some success in trying out Janet's advice. That is how she had snared Philip the one who looked like a horse, but Leonie was never one to like horses so that friendship was short-lived.

The doorbell rang. One night it would be the tall dark stranger who was to be her lover but tonight it would be Janet and Bill picking her up to take her to Jill's party across town. She checked her image in the mirror once more, grabbed her bag and coat and walked smartly to the front door, her heels clicking on the pine floor boards. She swung the door open. It was not Janet and Bill, it was a tall dark-haired young man. His features were rather bland and his eyes small. He was hardly 'handsome' she noticed.

He did not introduce himself. He simply said. 'Janet asked if I would pick you up. They wanted to get there especially early for some reason.' He looked directly at her as if completely unaware of the time and attention she had paid to make herself look good. He snapped in a matter-of-fact way. 'Are you ready?'

Leonie was irritated. She hated last minute changes. She had already planned the long conversation she was going to have with Janet in the car and now she was thwarted. Who did this chap think he was asking her if she was ready or not? Clearly, as she was standing there with her coat and bag in her hand, she was 'ready'. She stopped herself from snapping back a sarcastic reply, stepped forward so that he had to move back while she slammed the door shut.

'This way,' he said and walked ahead. Leonie clattered quickly behind him, struggling to keep up. She was not going to yell at him and ask him to walk more slowly. She would not lower herself. Her ankle twisted but when she righted herself she was fine. She straightened herself up hurriedly, ran a little and then continued to clatter quickly until, panting, she reached his car. If she had been in a better mood she would have noticed what a fine Mercedes it was but the way she felt now it could be a top notch sports car and she would not care. He swung open the passenger door and said:

'Get in.'

Leonie said nothing. The way she felt, she did not dare say anything. Head down so that she avoided meeting his eyes, she clambered into the passenger seat, pulling her coat and bag swiftly inside before he slammed the door shut. She sat rigidly, clutching her bag and coat closely to her stomach. Neither of them spoke all the way to Jill's house. She seethed inside, he whistled tunelessly as though he did not have a care in the world. He seemed completely oblivious to her existence.

He pulled into the parking space and leapt out of the car. He walked round to her side and opened the door. 'I'll give you a lift home too.' He said.

'You'll be lucky' she muttered to herself as she stumbled slightly on the rough pavement, trying to get to the party and other more amenable people as quickly as she could.

'Hi. Welcome you two' Jill called as they made their way to the open door. 'Glad you could make it Mike.'

'So Mike is his name' Leonie muttered to herself again, furious that he had not even bothered to tell her. Jill gave Leonie a hug 'Pleased to see you again

Leonie. Janet's inside dying to know how you two got on.'

Leonie's face was expressionless as she returned Jill's hug. She pulled out a box of chocolates from her bag, thrust them into Jill's hands and made a beeline through the throng of people to the back of the house.

She saw Janet deep in conversation with Bill. She would not interfere. She would wait.

'Drink?' a voice asked beside her. A glass was thrust into her hand and the owner of the voice poured her some red wine.

'Thanks' she sighed. 'I need this!'

'Oh?' the eyes that looked into hers were light blue.

'Yes, oh boy do I need this. The journey here was terrible. First of all…' Leonie was on a roll. She went into great deal about how her lift to the party was messed up and how she detested men who treated her like a piece of furniture. She left nothing to the imagination. Her listener's eyes sparkled. He was enjoying her tirade.

'What are you doing next Saturday?' he asked.

'Pardon?' Leonie stopped. Next Saturday was nothing to do with … She turned to look more closely at the speaker. No, he did not look like a horse or and his laugh did not sound like a snorting pig, in fact he looked quite handsome even if he was on the short side. 'Er nothing' she said meekly.

'Well,' he paused as if waiting for its effect. 'Well would you like to come to the theatre with me on Friday? There is a new play on. It's the first night but I know someone who has seen them in rehearsal and it is great and' his face lit up with a cheeky smile, ' I promise not to treat you like a piece of furniture.'

Leonie grinned and nodded. 'Maybe this time' she thought to herself.

RETURN TO WITCHES' MOUNTAIN
Gerry Wright

Three months had passed since early autumn, and it was time to visit Charlesburgh again. Rick drove along the valley road for this second visit as a field service engineer.

The highway was vaguely familiar but he was not concentrating on it. His thoughts were elsewhere. On his previous visit, many strange things had occurred and he was turning these over in his mind. Never before had he subscribed to ideas about the paranormal, but right now, he was not so sure. Outwardly, he rejected them, but at this moment, he thought back to those strange events - his meeting with Joe Kiley, dead these twenty years, and his phantom truck. His visit to the Black Ridge Motel and Restaurant and meeting Mack and Jenny, the proprietors – dead nearly as long and then of old Mabel, masquerading as a waitress, who had walked through a solid wall.

At the time, he had vowed never to return to this spot – Spiller Township – but then he had met Kitty, a real Southern Belle, he had decided, and as pretty as a picture, and strangely, the more he thought about her, the more he wanted to see her again. Why? he wondered. He had known many other attractive young women before. Perhaps it was her parting, 'Y'all come back now', in her lovely southern drawl, but maybe it really was the mountain, drawing him back.

Mountains reared either side of the two-lane valley highway, their slopes tree-covered, with pines, mostly, on the north facing slopes and deciduous trees on those facing south. Rick could see where clear-cutting for lumber had taken place in the areas of the pines and on the other side, bare, gaunt, leafless branches of the deciduous trees reached skywards. The higher peaks bore traces of snow. The valley was protected from the worst of the winter weather and the highway was clear of ice and snow. Mists drifted back and forth on the upper slopes as if a warning to unwanted visitors.

The further he drove, the stronger the feeling welled inside him to visit Spiller again. Was it really that damn mountain calling him? – no it couldn't be, he didn't believe in such things, he reminded himself. More likely, he thought, it was his wish to see beautiful Kitty again, so when he saw the sign on the right indicating the road up the mountain to Spiller, he took it. He drove the two miles or so to the small town where he decided he would pass the night. There was no way he was going to attempt to use the ridge road after dark – just in case!

He wondered if the town would be the same – things changed a lot around here and in a short time too. Would Kitty still be here? He hoped so.

He reached the town limits, where a sign announced, 'Welcome to Spiller Township. Altitude 3000 feet. Population 400'. At the bottom of the notice he read, 'Please drive carefully you may encounter problems from this point'. Rick smiled, 'You can say THAT again,' he said aloud. Then he saw the diner. It was just as he remembered - a neat and tidy log-built construction, with a dirt pull-in out front and on the side. 'Spiller Restaurant' said a sign over the door and front window, and then, underneath, 'Rooms for Rent'. That's handy, he thought. A good supper during the evening, a long chat with Kitty, if indeed she were still here, to find out more of the history and reputation of the mountain, and that altogether would be a time pleasantly spent. He would then tackle the ridge road the next day. He did not have to, he knew that, but something told him he must.

He pulled onto the dirt parking lot at the side of the building, stopped, killed the motor, and climbed out. Taking his briefcase and the bag containing a change of clothes from the trunk, he went into the diner. Dropping the bags onto the floor next to the reception desk, he rang the brass bell on the end of the counter for assistance. Then he looked around. The restaurant was the same, and, yes, there was the doorway in the wall close to the door to the kitchen area through which Mabel had walked and thence through the solid wall behind. The reception desk and all the furniture was of a dark polished wood and clearly maintained to a high standard.

Rick felt his spirits sink when a woman of around fifty appeared through the door behind the desk. She was a pleasant enough looking person, around five feet four and with dark hair. Somehow, she reminded him quite a lot, of Kitty. Maybe she was Kitty, and perhaps fate had brought him onto the mountain during a time that was, in fact, many years after his first visit – mountain-time that is. That would be a cruel blow. He overcame his disappointment and booked a room for the night with breakfast at eight thirty the next morning. There was no point in starting along the high route too early.

He ordered an evening meal for eight o'clock and then retired to his room, where, after showering, he waited, filling in time checking his documents and reading a newspaper he had picked up earlier. He took time out too, to look at the mountainside from the window of his room; it was a spectacular view and as he gazed upon it, he wondered what could have taken place here in the past, and what possibly could happen in the future. He was, after all, a stranger here, who had no real appreciation of the mountain, or indeed its possible latent powers.

Eight o'clock arrived, and he made his way down to the restaurant. It was empty and he noticed that one table had been laid for one person. He assumed it was for him. Moments later, the door from the kitchen opened and Kitty appeared. She looked even more attractive than he remembered, five feet four, long blonde hair tied back in a ponytail, little make-up and a good figure in her white blouse and tight fitting ankle length pants. Rick's spirits rose immediately.

Kitty gave him a broad smile, 'It's Rick, ain't it,' she said in that Southern drawl he remembered so well. 'You were here 'bout three months ago. Yeah?'

'That's right,' Rick confirmed happily. She had remembered his name, maybe a little too quickly, he thought. Perhaps she was glad he had returned and, in that case, the feeling was mutual. Rick ordered a pre-dinner Jack Daniels and sat on a stool at the bar, with the glass in front of him on the highly polished counter.

'You said you'd be back. Seems like it was a long time,' she said.

Rick smiled and sipped his drink, 'I seem to remember you told me to come back,' he said. She frowned.

'Y'all come back now,' he said attempting to mimic her Southern accent. She gave a laugh showing her perfect, white teeth, and her eyes brightened.

'Oh, that, I guess that's just a habit 'round here. Most folks say that.'

'It's very quiet tonight,' Rick noted, taking another sip, but not allowing his eyes to wander too far from the beautiful young woman before him.

'It's January and we don't get many here this time o' year. Maybe a few loggers, but they ain't working these woods so much these days.'

Kitty showed him the menu and he made his selection, chicken soup, followed by steak and vegetables. He would have a small beer with it and then decide on a dessert later. She went into the kitchen leaving him with just the aroma of her very pleasant perfume. She's beautiful, he thought, almost too good to be true. Then, the thought crossed his mind; maybe she is too good to be true. He put those thoughts away and waited for the meal.

When it arrived, he realised that this was real country cooking he had heard so much about - a large bowl of soup with fresh, home baked bread, and afterwards, a large steak and a pile of vegetables.

'I'll never sleep after this,' he said as Kitty placed the plate in front of him.

'Y'all do fine,' she replied.

'Is that another order?' They both laughed.

'If you're not busy, why don't you sit a while and we can talk,' he suggested.

'Really?'

'Yeah, really. Then you can tell me all about Spiller and the mountain.'

'Okay. I'll go get myself a coffee. It'll be nice to have someone to talk to.' She disappeared into the kitchen and came out a few minutes later with a large flask of coffee and a jug of cream.

'This will last us quite a long time,' she said. The longer the better, Rick thought.

Whilst he ate, Kitty told him many stories about Spiller and the mountain and many of them were very strange, even weird, but she was a girl born in the small town, and had lived there all her life. Things, which to Rick appeared weird, seemed not to worry Kitty very much. She confirmed that it was her mother he had seen when he arrived, and that her mother's married name was Kiley. Her father had been a trucker and had been killed in a crash on the mountain when his truck went off the road. Rick suppressed a gasp, he knew the story already, but he couldn't possibly let on. Perhaps Kitty hadn't been told her father had been two-timing his wife and that's what had led to his untimely end.

The longer they talked and drank coffee together, the more Rick was drawn to her, as if it were an irresistible magnetism. A moth to a flame!

He decided to turn in around ten thirty. Kitty stood very close to him as he prepared to leave the restaurant. Her perfume and aura almost held him captive. He wanted to take her in his arms and kiss her goodnight. He felt that she too, almost expected it. He was aware of what signals he must be giving off. However, he had always considered himself to be a gentleman, and he should treat this Southern Belle like a lady, so he leaned forward and gave her a light kiss on the cheek. She lifted her face to receive it and smiled.

'Good night Rick,' she said, in a soft, gentle voice. Rick was finding his breathing becoming rather labored.

'Good night, Kitty. Thanks for a delicious meal and a lovely evening.'

'You're welcome honey,'

He opened the door to go to the stairs, and turned and again said, 'Good night.'

'Y'all come back for breakfast, now,' she said with a laugh.

'You bet,' he called back as he walked up the stairs to his room.

Rick awoke, well rested, the next morning after a surprisingly good night's sleep, after the large supper he had eaten. He had wakened sometime during the night to find a full moon shining through his window where he had left the curtains partly open. The room was comfortable. Not too cold, even with the outside winter temperature, nor too warm with the central heating. He had gone to sleep thinking of Kitty and he woke up with her still on his mind. He took his time showering and shaving, and then went down to breakfast around eight.

A dense fog was lying across the mountainside and so he decided that he would not hurry to leave, but would give it time to clear. Leaving later would also give him the opportunity to see Kitty again and talk more with her. He still couldn't quite understand just how much, and why, she had invaded his thoughts.

Kitty was there to serve his breakfast, full of smiles; bright as a button, he thought. What a great start to the day for me. Breakfast consisted of country sized helping of grits, followed by ham, two eggs over easy and pancakes, all served up with toast and butter. To complete the meal there was a large flask of coffee, black, no sugar, for him and plenty more if he needed it. He was sure that Kitty would not have served other guests quite like this. Perhaps it was the peck on the cheek last night with a promise of what might happen sometime in the future. Whatever it was, Rick was not going to complain. In addition, Kitty sat on a chair at the table next to his and prepared to continue their conversation of the previous evening. Her white blouse was open an extra button at the top and the rest of her rig showed her off to her very best. Everything to make a man drool. I'm on Witches' Mountain being bewitched, Rick thought as he tried to eat his meal and gaze at her at the same time. Maybe she's a witch herself – but I really don't care, she's fabulous. Moth to a flame!

The fog was clearing slowly by ten thirty, so after several coffees and a long enjoyable talk with Kitty, he decided it was time to leave. He needed to be in Charlesburgh by noon, do his business, stay overnight and then return the next day to Spiller and of course Kitty, and stay overnight again.

She saw him to the door.

'Will you be coming back here?' she asked, in a voice which Rick thought clearly was a hopeful one.

'Of course. Day after tomorrow. Can I reserve a room?'

'Of course you can,' she replied and her face lit up. 'Shall I keep that same room for you? It's about the best one we have.'

'That'd be nice. I liked that room.'

124

'It's just down the hall from mine,' she said. Rick's pulse beat a little faster.

'See you the day after tomorrow then,' he said and leaned towards her. This time he didn't give her a peck on the cheek. This time it was a soft kiss on the lips. She didn't pull back and Rick felt he was welcome. Through his half closed eyes he saw her eyes were closed and he realised she was leaning close to him. He stepped back, but only slowly; she was smiling and it was at that point, Rick noticed how green her eyes were.

'Until the day after tomorrow then,' he said softly in a somewhat husky voice.

'Day after tomorrow,' she repeated in agreement and in an equally soft and husky tone. 'Don't be late.'

'No way,' he said, gazing directly into her eyes and not wanting to break the spell.

Any early morning frost had gone off the car and all he had to do was clean off the melted water from the windows. He started the motor and sat with the door open until the demister had cleared the windshield inside. Kitty stood waiting at the door as he left and he kept his eyes firmly on her until all the windows of the car were clear, then he engaged drive and slowly pulled out of the parking lot. Kitty waved him goodbye until he disappeared round the first bend up the lower slopes of the mountain.

The road up was steep until reaching a point where it turned left, it ran along the ridge more or less parallel to the summit of the ridge and the road far below in the valley. As he drove, the mist became intermittent, with clear intervals and then patches of fog as they drifted across the slopes prior to breaking up.

He reached a point where the road rounded a right hand bend and where he could see he was about to run into another fog bank, when he heard the loud sound of a bull-horn ahead of him. Suddenly, around the bend and out of the fog, a large, old Kenworth truck appeared, on Rick's side of the road and heading straight for him. There was nothing to do except head for the verge at the side of the road, where there was a spillway, designed to take melt-water off the mountain quickly and help to reduce erosion, at the side of the road. The horn sounded a long blast, increasing in volume as it got closer, as the truck, piled high with logs, roared passed.

'Son-of-a-bitch!' shouted Rick, as he pulled the wheel hard over, and ran off the road, over the edge of the steep-sided water run-off. Thankfully, there was no water in rock-strewn bottom of it. Angrily, he turned round in his seat to see where the truck was. The road was clear. No truck. No logs. No sound.

'Son-of-a-bitch!' he yelled again. He thumped the steering wheel with both hands. 'Kiley, you bastard!' he said aloud, his subconscious confirming what the rest of his brain refused to accept. 'Kiley, I'll get you!' then he grimaced, realizing how stupid and futile his threat was. If it had been Joe Kiley driving the truck, Rick could never 'get him', Kiley being dead these twenty years and all.

Rick had been so eager in his attempt to avoid what he felt sure was a real truck not an apparition, but not entirely sure, that he had lost sense of his ensuing actions. The car was sitting at an angle across the steep side of the ditch, with its front fender partially dug into the soft grit and larger stones, which surrounded the boulders at the bottom and on the other side. He knew there must be some damage and he needed to see how much. He selected reverse and stepped on the pedal – nothing happened except the motor raced and the rear wheels threw up a ton of grit and stones behind. He tried again with the same result.

He turned off the motor, and with difficulty climbed out. He slammed the door and kicked the side of the car in frustration – he didn't feel any better! Then he went round to the trunk, took out his overnight bag and then pushed any important papers he needed from his brief case, into it. He looked around the vehicle – it was well and truly jammed into the loose grit and gravel, there was only one way to move it – he needed a tow-truck. He slammed the trunk as well and then angrily gave the rear wheel a final kick – it did not make him feel any better! Using the remote, he locked the doors and then throwing the carrying strap of his bag over his shoulder, set off on foot, back down the mountainside.

The journey back to Spiller was around two miles, as the crow flies, or more properly in this part of the country, as the eagle flies, but because of the gradient of the slope and the hairpin bends traversing back and forth, the journey was more like four. During his trek down the rough road, Rick had one of those arguments it is possible to have with oneself from time to time.

'Why the hell did I come this way?'
'You had to!'
'Why?'

'Think about it, buddy. Two things called you and you simply HAD to come.'

'What two things? I know Kitty was the one I wanted to see.'

'The mountain, buddy, the mountain. You had to come. Don't ask me why. You just had to come. You didn't have a choice.'

'You're crazy!'

'No, YOU'RE crazy.'

This was a stupid argument, Rick could not rationalize what had happened on the one hand – on the other, and he had the strange feeling his other self knew it was true. Never argue with yourself, you never win, he thought and carried on down the mountain. Anyway, Kitty was down there. Maybe every cloud DOES have a silver lining.

He arrived back at the Spiller Restaurant, 'With Rooms to Let', around three in the afternoon. He rang the bell on the reception desk. His luck was in. Kitty came from the back. Her mouth fell open.

'Rick,' she said in surprise. 'What are you doing here? Is everything all right? Are you okay? Let me get you a drink.' She poured him a beer and he proceeded to tell her what had happened. He told her about the truck but made no mention of his fears that it was a phantom and that her dead father, Joe Kiley, was driving it.

'The truck was headed downhill coming this way,' he said.

'No trucks have been in Spiller today. It must have turned off somewhere in the woods. But that's strange; they ain't cutting trees here this year.'

128

Rick drank his beer and found himself again concentrating on Kitty's lovely green eyes. Okay, Kiley, maybe you did me a favor, was the thought that passed through his mind.

'I'll phone Mickey Jackson down the road a piece,' she said. 'He has a tow truck – used to do a lot of business at one time, but not now. I guess he'll be glad to help you out.'

She made the call, explaining where the car was. Mickey was glad to do the job and he said he would let Rick know what the situation was.

There was nothing left to do, but sit and wait.

'Is that room still available for tonight?' he asked.

She gave him that broad smile of hers. 'Of course it is honey. I wouldn't have let it if you were coming back the day after tomorrow like you said.'

Dusk was beginning to fall when Mickey rang in with his report. There was some slight damage, which must be fixed before he could drive it, but he would work on the car and it would be ready around late morning the next day. Rick was happy. He did not mention to anyone that he would be happy if it even took three days.

Kitty served his Jack Daniels and later his supper. They sat and talked during and after it. The 'good night' kiss was not a peck on the cheek like that of the previous night, and it was longer and warmer than that of the morning when he had left. He turned in around ten thirty, and exhausted, soon fell asleep with Kitty once more to the forefront of his thoughts.

Rick awoke with a start about twelve thirty, he thought, but he really did not know. What he did know was something felt very different. The room was cold – unnaturally cold. It was obvious to him that the central heating was not working. He turned his head to check the time on the digital clock on the bedside table with its illuminated read-out. It was black. He reached out to turn on the lamp on the bedside table – nothing. The power's off. There was a full moon that night and a small amount of light coming through the gap between the curtains. Then the room lightened as the moon shone brightly after a cloud had passed across its face. Moments passed and the air grew even colder.

He was trying to get to sleep, when he heard a faint noise at the door. At first, he ignored it. Then he heard it again and the door opened slowly and quietly. He watched and Kitty's face, lit by the moonlight and almost a deathly pale appeared from around the door and he heard a very quiet, frightened voice, almost like a little girl's, call out.

'Rick, Rick. Are you awake?' she called softly.

'Yeah,' he replied.

'Can I come in?'

Things were not right somehow, Rick knew that. The thought of having Kitty in his bedroom was certainly appealing, but even he, as a person who would deny things of a paranormal nature, realized that not everything was well in the house and even, maybe, Spiller Township.

'Sure you can, honey,' he said, in an as reassuring tone as he could.

As she crossed the room from the door to the bed, she passed through the shaft of bright moonlight again, and he could see that she was wearing a dressing gown over what he assumed were pajamas. She lifted the bedcovers on the other side of Rick and slid under them. As she tried to settle, Rick realized she was shaking violently.

'You're cold, honey,' he said, reaching out to put his arm around her. She didn't stop him.

'No, I'm not cold.'

'What is it then?'

'I'm scared. Scared as hell.'

'Why, what's the problem?'

'It's the Mountain.'

'What do you mean?'

It seems to have happened at regular intervals. My Granma seems to know about these things. Nobody's ever said, but I've thought all along that she has the 'talent' as they refer to it.'

'Talent?'

'Yeah. I think she might be a witch or something. She has told me strange stories about the Mountain. Whenever it happens, Mom has been here and we stay close together at night. In the past, some people who have been on their own have died of no apparent cause. Mom has always said that to be sure that you're safe, you have to be close by someone.'

'What about tonight? Where's your Mom?'

'Mom has had to go over to Granma's. I can't be with her, and I'm scared. I don't want to die of no apparent cause.'

'You won't, honey,' Rick said, and pulled her shaking body closer to him. 'I won't let anyone or anything, harm you.' She snuggled close and pulled the covers up over their heads. Rick suddenly raised his head.

'Do you hear a train somewhere way off? There's a roaring sound and I thought I heard a train whistle blow.'

'It's the Mountain,' Kitty said, still shaking with fear. 'It makes that sort of noise when something bad is going to happen.'

The moonlight across the room seemed to falter and Rick heard a flapping noise outside the window as it flickered. He held Kitty close to him, trying to comfort and reassure her. She clung to him for support. They kissed each other as their closeness became contact and their passions were aroused.

There may have been something weird and paranormal taking place outside the window, but something very natural and human gradually pushed it, and the fear of it, into the background. Kitty's cries of fear were replaced by an entirely different cry as they made love. To hell with what's going on out there, Rick thought, this ain't no phantom event, and not too long afterwards, the pair confirmed it as they enjoyed each other again.

As they lay in each other's arms, they realized that the train noises had ceased as had the flapping noises outside the window. The digital clock came back on and showed three thirty. Strange, Rick thought, normally the figures flash until you re-set them. The light in the hallway outside the room showed through the gap under the door and the room was beginning to feel warm again.

'We're safe now,' Kitty said as she snuggled even deeper into Rick's embrace. Moments later, they were peacefully asleep in each other's arms.

Rick awoke around seven. It was still dark. He reached for Kitty, but she was not there. Had he dreamed everything? Then he turned on the light and saw that the pillow next to his was dented and there were a couple of loose, blonde hairs lying where her head had lain.

He showered and shaved, and was down in the dining room by seven forty five. Kitty came in. They looked at each other intently, and then she came to him. They embraced and kissed and as she stepped back and smiled, Rick could see tears beginning to well in her eyes.

'Are you okay?' he enquired concerned. She smiled again and nodded.

'I'm fine, absolutely fine,' she stated and stepped forward and kissed him again.

'I'm sorry if I...' he began. There was no way, realistically, he could blame what had happened on a phantom train whistle – or could he - but she put her fingers on his lips.

'No.' she said, 'Everything was fine then and it is fine now. Believe me. Now sit down and I'll bring your breakfast.'

Breakfast was over by nine thirty and Mickey Jackson had brought the car, still damaged but perfectly roadworthy. At ten o'clock, Rick was ready to leave, albeit unwillingly, but he had a job to do. He needed the money. He had to pay the alimony. What a pity he had not met Kitty years earlier.

She went to the car with him. They held each other and kissed more. Kitty told him that an old man from Spiller had died the night before. He had been healthy and showed no outward signs of a cause of death – but Rick heard he had been alone.

'I'm sure you saved my life being with me last night,' she said and hugged him again.

'You probably saved mine too,' he said, and then added, 'You're the best thing that's ever happened to me, Kitty. I'll see you the day after tomorrow, like I said before.'

'Promise?' she asked.

'Cross my heart and hope to die,' he said more seriously than ever before and meaning it more than ever before. 'And when I get back, you and I have something very important to talk over.'

She smiled, 'Really?'

'You better believe it, honey,' he said and kissed her again.

He climbed into the car but before he could close the door, she leaned in, looked him straight in the eye and smiled. 'Y'all come back now,' she said softly.

'You can bet a million bucks on it, and there'll be a lot to talk about.' She pulled back and Rick closed the door. Then he opened the window. She leaned on the windowsill.

'I love you Rick,' she said with a smile on her face and the start of tears in her eyes.

'I love you too, Baby,' he said with conviction, 'I love you too. See you the day after tomorrow.' Then he engaged drive and pulled slowly out onto the mountain road, knowing in his uttermost being that the previous night was merely the beginning of the rest of his life. There was no way, he decided, he could live without her, and the day after tomorrow could not come soon enough.

The Vagrant
Gerry Wright

Spring came late to the small East Midlands market town and with it, no one quite knew precisely when, came Joe 'The Vagrant', as everyone referred to him. The town was in a very affluent area and his appearance upset and embarrassed many of the well-off local residents. Never before could anyone remember such a scruffy character being there.

People crossed the street to avoid him whenever they saw him approaching. No one wanted to associate with him, after all, this was a well to-do-place; nearly everyone was employed in the professions in the nearby city, even the shops were of the above-average type and only stocked the best and most expensive goods.

Joe, on the other hand, looked different. His old, battered grey trilby hat had seen better days. The brown overcoat he always wore was threadbare and tied at the waist with an old, brown leather belt; brown trousers matched his coat. His black boots appeared very old and trodden down at the heels, but if anyone had taken the trouble to look more closely, they would have seen that those almost-worn-out boots were clean, as was the rest of his attire. A scarf, knotted at his throat, covered whatever he wore beneath his coat. His collar-length dark hair was liberally streaked with grey and he sported, if sported were the appropriate word, a beard that matched. Although long, both hair and beard were tidily kept.

No one knew from whence he came or where he spent his nights. They cared little, as long as it was nowhere near their properties.

'A rogue,' one said.

'An ex-convict, I'll be bound,' another suggested.

'Up to no good, that's for sure,' someone else pontificated. 'Perhaps he'll be gone soon.'

No one ever approached Joe; he was not only a vagrant but also an outcast. It was true, no one had checked him out for leprosy, but that was how they all treated him.

Little Peter Clifford, a lad of five years, in his innocence, saw things a little differently. He had seen Joe at closer quarters than anyone else in the town.

'I think he's Santa Claus in disguise,' he told his mother. She of course, was aghast that he had been so close to Joe, and ordered him to stay away from him; 'he just could not be trusted', and 'sometimes men like him could whisk away little boys and they would never see their parents again', she had said. This had frightened Peter and although he had bad dreams, Joe was always the good man. Peter, in fact, was the only person in the town who had actually looked into Joe's bright, blue eyes and, without understanding, seen the care, which shone in them. He could not imagine him as bad as all the people thought, but mother's word was law and sadly, he kept his distance whenever he saw Joe approaching. Joe for his part was saddened too but not surprised; this had happened in other places before. It could have been not only his appearance but also his very strange limping gait.

People were surprised that Joe stayed for so long. He was seen in some of the older parts of the town standing and looking around him. A woman reported in one of the local shops that she had seen him 'wiping his eyes and possibly tears from them,' as she put it. There was something very strange about Joe, but no one could quite 'put their finger on it', but he was never reckoned to be a real threat to anyone.

Spring faded into summer, and summer into autumn and a chill came with it. Joe still came to the town. Those traders who felt sorry for him would give him menial tasks to do and pay him a pittance. The cold was affecting him and they noticed it. On one occasion when toting for work, he approached a large house in a leafy avenue and asked the occupant, an old woman in her eighties, if he could clear her garden of fallen leaves.

'Thank you, yes,' she said, and later, whilst paying him, she studied him very closely.

'You look familiar,' she said in a suspicious tone. 'Have you ever been in trouble here? I never forget a face. In all my years as a magistrate, I have never forgotten a troublemaker.'

'No ma'am,' he replied, politely and in a quiet voice, 'I've never been in trouble here.'

'Hm... Well you be careful,' she advised.

'Yes, ma'am, I'll be careful.'

Winter came and the temperatures fell. It was one of the coldest winters in living memory. Joe's visits to the town became less frequent and then people realised he had not appeared for several days and they began to think he had moved on. They were glad that perhaps he had, but somehow he left a gap.

One morning, the phone rang in the local Police Station.

'We've found Joe,' a local farmer reported, 'in one of our old barns some way from the farm. He's dead.'

The townsfolk knew that, at last, Joe the Vagrant had finally gone.

The pathologist later revealed that he had died from hypothermia. No crime had been committed, but whilst carrying out the examination, he had discovered that Joe had lost both legs below the knees and he had been fitted with artificial limbs. That explained the strange gait.

The Police searched his possessions. A few very old letters indicated that many years earlier Joe had lived in the town, in a part now entirely redeveloped. They also found, in an inside pocket of his overcoat, two small cardboard boxes, one containing a Victoria Cross, the other a Military Cross. Papers in his old rucksack confirmed that they had been awarded to him for deeds of heroism and valour in the face of the enemy.

The news stunned the whole population of the town. Joe was a hero, a local hero, in fact; the old magistrate's memory was indeed very good.

'Why, on earth,' someone voiced, 'had no one asked some questions before?'

Their collective shame was palpable, particularly when the vicar, in the funeral service, used the text 'He came to his own and his own received him not.'

OTHER ANTHOLOGIES PUBLISHED BY WORDPLAY

Precinct Murder
by Various Authors

New York: the city where killers never sleep. For those that like their murder stories potted, this is the perfect coffee table crime anthology.

WordPlay ShowCase
by Various Authors

A collection of works by a series of writers, for some of whom this represents their first time in print. The anthology covers a whole range of writing: factual, fiction, social commentary, and poetry.

Shorts for Autumn
by Various Authors

The winner of the 2012 Writing Magazine Writers' Circle Anthology of the Year award, this is the ideal accompaniment to an autumn evening spent by the fire, or that coffee break when you need to unwind and relax. For all fans of short fiction.

Made in the USA
Charleston, SC
06 January 2014